Second Chance *at Christmas*

Also by Emily Engberts

As Emmy Engberts (YA romance)
Her Elysium (Flowers and Keyboards 1)
The Other Dress (Flowers and Keyboards 2)

As E. Engberts (YA scifi)
BASE Status: Online

As Skylar Heart (18+)
Shattered
Unraveled

As Rosa Swann (18+)
Mated to the Alpha Serial
The Baby Pact Trilogy
Second Chance Mates Serial
Making a Family Serial
Omegas' Destined Alpha Serial
The Vampire's Past Trilogy

Second Chance

at

Christmas

Emily Engberts

1

Sanne

The sea around the ferry is grey, like the sky. The slow waves roll over the Wadden Sea, much calmer than on the North Sea side of the island, and in the distance I can see the dikes appear as the ferry turns. It's Friday afternoon, usually one of the busiest times on the ferry, but today the boat feels as empty as I do.

I watch some students as they get their early drink on with cheap beer. Something they'll probably continue doing at the only bar on the island the moment they've dumped their bags at the house they're renting. And then there are the exhausted looking students, likely on their way home to see their parents and other family members after being away to university for months.

I wasn't supposed to go on this holiday on my own. It was supposed to be a celebration of being together with my girlfriend of four years, I was going to propose to her. But then, three months ago, she said that she wasn't feeling it anymore, that the relationship didn't work for her anymore and that she wanted to start living her own life. It had been such a shock, within days, she'd moved out and left me alone in the apartment we used to share, the apartment we chose together.

I grieved, but then I got over it, I thought so, anyway. Until this holiday came around and cancelling it was not going to happen as it was going to cost me extra money, which I don't have right now. I also realised that I really did need to get away from everything and a week on Schiermonnikoog sounded like a perfect plan. The holiday apartment was paid for, the boat tickets were paid for and I had blocked off the free days anyway. Not going didn't make any sense.

So, here I am, sitting in the belly of a ferry, waiting until it arrives at the island so I can get to my home for the week. The excitement hasn't set in yet, but I'm pretty sure that it will soon. I hope anyway.

There is something special about islands, no matter how non-exotic they are. Just being surrounded by the vast sea, the silence, the emptiness. It clears my head in ways that few things ever do.

I watch people around me stand up, grabbing their things and putting on their coats. The ferry is almost there. I look out the window, the island is so much closer now.

The mudflat side of the island is just a long row of dikes, with some dunes on either side, and I can see the trees and some houses over the dikes. Three buses are coming down the pier, filled with the people who are leaving, and they'll be waiting to pick up the new travellers.

The ferry bounces abruptly as it finally falls still against the pier and I stand up, grabbing my bags as I get to the exit.

The wind cuts into my cheeks as I leave the warmth and safety of the ferry and get out onto the pier. I drag my bags behind me. The salty air is cold as I've never felt it before and it's almost like my nose is starting to freeze from the inside out. I've never been on one of the islands while it was this cold and when I look over at the pier, I can see ice stacking on the side of it. That's... I've never seen that before.

As I locate the bus to the right stop, I pay for a ticket, cash because that's all they accept, and sit down in a seat. For such a small island, they still somehow manage to have four busses for each boat that arrives. I shiver from the residual cold, only slowly warming up again.

Then I watch over the mudflats as the bus drives onto

the island.

I nod at the lady who gave me the key of the apartment I'm in for the week, not sure what else I can do at her fast words. She seems sweet and she's definitely trying to be helpful.

I open the door to the apartment, finding it a little… old? Everything looks well cared for, and I'm sure some things are brand new, but the colour scheme is definitely not something you'd still expect these days. So much brown and so many wooden elements, definitely no longer in style.

When I booked this place, I thought it looked charming. I imagined spending a couple of days with my ex here, cuddled up in front of the fake fire and not having to worry about anything. Now it just feels so grandma-y, not as much fun, especially since I'm alone.

I drop my bags in the bedroom, checking the windows for drafts, since it's a little chilly in here, but I can't find any. Probably just not heated up yet.

I definitely need to hunt down the thermostat first, get the temperature up a little. And after that, I guess it's a good idea to get some food in the house and probably go out to the sea.

The thing I'm looking forward to the most right now is seeing the sea, going out onto that beach and walk up to the waves. Only, the stores here close early, so I really do need to get some dinner in before I do anything else.

Although…

I remember that the bar here had pretty good food. Although, that may just have been my experience as a broke and drunk teenager. I don't know. That very easily possible. But I also don't know if I want to try out another place to eat today. I think I may need some booze with my food tonight, and the Tox Bar seems like a great place for that. It used to be *the* place to be when I was a teenager. The booze wasn't too expensive and they stayed open until late. That, and it was the only place on the island where they didn't look at you weirdly for being under the age of forty or something, at least in the eyes of my 18-year-old self.

I dig in my bag and pull out a nicer pair of jeans and then a warm wool sweater in black with dark grey elements, which I know suits me well. Even if I don't need to impress anyone, I can at least look nice, just for myself. I pull my hair into a ponytail, and then check myself in the mirror. I look a little red, probably from the cold wind as I came here, but for the first time in weeks, I feel like there is a spark in my eyes.

Coming here was the right idea. Definitely!

I slip into a sturdy pair of low heels, zipping the boots up, and then put on my long jacket. I get cold so easily, some people, like my ex, used to joke that I should live in a warmer climate, not in the Netherlands, but I also don't deal with heat well, so I don't think it would work out.

I grab my wallet, a small bag and the key of this place. Then I step outside and pull the door closed behind me. The wind is icy and cuts into my cheeks even more than when I stepped off the ferry, so so cold. The forecast said that it's going to get even colder this week, that we may even be able to ice skate during Christmas, which hasn't happened in years. I don't often go ice skating, but I still love it and I know that there is going to be a rink not too far down the road. Important research.

I pull my jacket around me tighter as I walk down the road into town. The place I'm in is about halfway between the town and the beach. Which is great when you want to go to the beach, but when it's cold like this, it's not as much fun to brace the cold to get something to eat from town.

As I walk past the houses, the Christmas lights are on in some of them, though many of the houses are dark, probably not rented out for the winter. Which seems to be common. I walk past a large and very impressive looking hotel, and then an 'evening store' which means it's open until nine in the evening. On the island, that's seen as an evening store, and for a place where shops close at five or six the latest, it's open quite late. To go from a city to an island like here, it's an interesting experience.

As a teen, I thought it was annoying that stores weren't open late enough, and that the only real bar around here didn't let people in after two in the evening. But that was in the summer months, and I'd spend my days between being drunk and being hungover for not an insignificant number of weeks every year. At the time, I thought that that was the best way to spend my summer holidays, and looking back, I don't disagree. Although, maybe not being *that* drunk would have been a good idea too...

I come to a three way crossing and take the turn to the right, in front of me is one of the three clothing stores that the island has. Although, I'm pretty sure this is one of those 'living place stores' where you can buy clothes and also buy things for in your house and such. I don't know, all the stores here seem to be like that, they'll have like two or three different elements to them. They'll sell clothes and home things, or clothes and being the local drugstore, or they're the local book store, but they're also the only toy store around. I guess that with an island this small, which mostly depends on the holiday seasons to keep surviving, this is a sensible thing to do. But I still find it odd, and you never know where to find things.

On my right side is the church behind a large hedge, which is bare without its leaves, as I take another left turn, walking into the 'main street' of the island. This is the main road where the only supermarket is at, and the tourist information office, and, of course, the place I'm going for, the Tox Bar. The place of many a drunk night and *interesting* teenage experiences.

First I walk past the whale jaws that are right across the street from the supermarket. The big blue whale jaws as impressive as ever and I stop to look at them for a few moments. I'm pretty sure there are pictures of me kissing some summer fling under them, the booze and warm summer nights making us do silly things. With how drunk most teens were during the summers, I guess that the lack of cars on this island really helped with there not being too many deadly drunk accidents. There's only so much damage you can do with a bike...

I walk on, finally slipping into the Tox Bar, my eyes scanning the large tables and then settling on a seat that isn't too out in the open and is pretty close to a window, so I can distract myself by looking outside.I'm with my back to a wall and can see everyone coming in. I put my jacket over the back of my chair and then make myself comfortable, rubbing my hands together, trying to get some sensations into them. I blow into my hands, trying to get them to warm up again.

A smiling waiter comes over, holding a writing block in

his hand as he hands me the menu. "Do you know what you'd like to drink?"

"I'd like a gluhwein." Mulled wine, tacky, maybe a little, but I'm cold and in the mood for doing something a little silly.

"One gluhwein coming up." He walks off again.

When I open the menu, looking at the different items on it, trying to figure out what I'm in the mood for, my eyes catch movement over the top of it and I don't know why, but I can't help but look up.

Sitting down a few tables over is a woman who looks somehow familiar. Her long brown hair is caught under a black knitted hat, which she's taking off right as I'm watching her. She's all dressed in brown, which could be dull, but not in this colour. This is the brow-red of fall, the colour of chestnuts and fallen leaves. A colour you'd want to wrap yourself in in front of a fire with a cup of hot chocolate, or maybe some cheese and gluhwein.

Then the woman looks up and I'm caught in her pale blue eyes, pale blue eyes I've seen very close up before and I immediately know who she is. Josie, the girl with white hair with streaks of every rainbow colour possible. Josie, the girl who'd wear super short shorts with army boots and a t-shirt that would show off her smooth stomach. Josie, the girl whose freckles I'd count and who I secretly kissed in the dunes.

That Josie had just sat down at a table and she's looking right at me too.

2

❄

Josie

It's freezing cold and the island is almost deserted, but I'm still glad I'm here instead of being at home and preparing for yet another Christmas dinner with my family. My family is generally nice, but when you're thirty and you still live on your own and you spend more time walking your dog and curling up with romance novels than going out and finding a 'partner', their looks and questions do get annoying.

So, this year, I decided to do my own thing and booked an apartment on Schiermonnikoog for the holiday. This way I can spend a whole week doing what I love most, walking the beaches and forests with my dog Bente and then curl up under a pile of blankets and read romance novels on my ereader. To me, this is almost as perfect as perfection can get, especially in the winter months.

What I hadn't counted on was running into someone I knew once. A girl who I never forgot. Sanne was the bright and always smiling girl from our group of summer friends. She was always laughing and we had such a great time, including many stolen kisses, over a number of summers. Sure, I knew that I was into girls. I don't know if she realised yet that she was too, but I definitely knew. Sure, we all had boyfriends back in the day, that's just what was normal during the summer, but I never really thought anything of it. The boys weren't for me, at least not for longer than a fling, but that didn't mean that it hadn't been fun.

I glance away for a moment, still surprised to see her here. She's grown up really well. Her mid-brown hair now has some shimmer under the lights, which tells me that she's probably got grey hairs, she's gotten older, as have I. Her style is simple, a warm black woollen sweater with some pattern on it that could be Scandinavian or something, I don't know. She's not wearing any jewellery, not even a wedding ring, and she wears her hair in a bun, away from her face, as she always used to do.

Bente pushes against my leg, making me return my attention to her. She looks up at me with her beautiful dark brown eyes in her black masked face with her white snout. She's a Stabyhoun, a very popular dog race in the northern provinces, and the sweetest dog you'll ever meet. And the best snuggling companion, with her fluffy fur and her easygoing personality.

"Yeah, sweetie, I'll ask for some water for you. We can't forget that." I pet her head and she pushes against my hand, looking at me.

Then I glance to Sanne, her eyes dart my way for a moment, before she looks away again. Then I see the waiter bring her a single glass with a dark red liquid in it. She's not waiting for anyone, she's here on her own too, or she wouldn't have ordered yet, right?

I don't know, it feels bad to just leave her on her own, especially since we've obviously recognised each other. Maybe I should go over to her... I may have come to the island to be on my own, but eating by myself, even with Bente at my side, isn't the most fun, and Sanne looks lonely.

"What do you think, girl?" But Bente just looks up at me happily, always ready for anything.

I slowly get up, leaving my things for now, and then go over to Sanne's table. "Hey." I feel so awkward, like we're teens again.

"Hey." Sanne smiles, her eyes lighting up. "Josie, right?" Though, I'm pretty sure she remembers me, the way her cheeks flare tells me she does.

"Yeah. You're Sanne, right?"

She nods. "Interesting to see you here too. Are you here by yourself, or are you waiting for someone?" She looks around, as I'd done before.

"I'm here with my girl." I nod down towards Bente.

As Sanne sees Bente her eyes start to sparkle and she breaks out in a big smile. "Oh, how cute. What's her name? Can I pet her?"

"Her name is Bente, and yes, you can pet her. She's very friendly." Bente, of course, immediately gets close to Sanne and puts her wet and dirty nose to Sanne's black jeans and I manage to not wince too much. They were nice and clean before, and there is now a brown blotch of dirt on them.

Sanne laughs and leans down to hug Bente more, who gets really excited by it all. Watching them gives me butterflies in my stomach, and it brings back memories of when Sanne and I used to spend time together, long summer nights near the sea.

Then Sanne looks up, eyeing my table. "If you're by yourself, do you want to join me?" She smiles in a way I can't ignore.

"Yeah. S-sure." Why do I feel like a stumbling teen all over again? "Let me just..." I motion at the stuff at my old table.

"Of course." She nods. "Do you need me to hold her for a moment?" She looks at Bente.

"If you could." I give her the leash and then quickly grab my jacket and bag from my own table. When I sit down in the chair opposite Sanne, Bente sits down between us all happily. Her nose going from one to the other, asking for petting the whole time. "What are you drinking? Red wine?"

Sanne smiles shyly, her cheeks pinking. "Gluhwein."

"Ah. A good idea." I look up, trying to get the attention of one of the waiters. When he comes over, I also order a gluhwein, and he gives me a menu. I eye the items on the menu, not sure what I really want to choose. "What are you ordering?" I glance up and catch Sanne staring at me, her cheeks going even pinker.

"I don't know yet." She looks down at her menu. "There is so much choice, and I have no idea what's good or anything."

"Their steaks are usually good. If you're into fish, you can do that, it's really fresh. And they have a winter stew that tastes *so* good." I shrug a little. "I come here regularly." If I go out to eat on the island, when I'm here with Bente, this is one of the places I frequent. Partially out of nostalgia, but also because it's just a good place to go, and they're open really late so it doesn't matter if I went for a walk that took way too long or if I got lost in a book again.

The waiter comes back with my gluhwein, but we wave him away again until we've decided what we want to eat. And it's not like there are many other people so it doesn't take long if we do finally order. There are only two other people, at one of the tables at the front part of the restaurant, I saw them when I came in.

"So, tell me..." Sanne looks at me. "Do you do this often? Come here on your own?"

I nod. "I like the island. And when you're outside of the holiday seasons, it's great to walk here with Bente and get away from it all for a couple of days."

"Of course." She nods.

"You don't do this very often?"

She shakes her head, her eyes going down, averting her gaze. "I don't. I wasn't..."

"It's okay. It's not for everyone." I instinctively reach out to her, wanting to put my hand on hers, but then I quickly pull it back. Just because we used to be friends doesn't mean that we can do this now. That was then, this is now.

"And then there was this woman with this really tiny dog..." I shake my head, grinning. "She wanted to know if I also did trimming, you know, hair and nails and such, because her previous vet did that..." I take another sip from the glass of gluhwein. I'm sure we've drank more than a whole bottle of this stuff by now. We're onto our desserts, pieces of steaming hot apple pie with whipped cream in front of us. Things were a little awkward at the start, but after a couple of minutes, we went back to how we used to be. Laughing, joking around.

"And, what did you tell her?" Sanne leans forward, her cheeks a little red from the warmth, or from the alcohol, probably both.

"I told her that we're a more rural veterinary, we don't tend to do things like that. But that I could ask around to see if I knew someone who could give her little dog a new haircut."

"And?" Impatient.

"She didn't seem to appreciate it." I shrug. "I don't know. But she shouldn't have moved out to the outskirts of the city if she wanted an all-in-one experience at her vet." I take another piece of the apple pie. I should be be leaving in not too long, Bente needs to stretch her legs and get her dinner too. Not that I want to leave…

Sanne shrugs too. "Yeah. That's the difference when you're at an expensive rich neighbourhood vet or one where dogs the size of calves also go to. And maybe the neighbourhood goat." She grins. Her smiles and attention on me keep my heart beating a little faster than normal, making me feel special.

Bente moves at our feet, putting her head on my lap, getting a little restless. I reach out to her, petting her head. "Yeah, yeah. We're leaving soon."

Sanne's eyes grow and she looks under the table. "Of course, she needs to eat too. Poor girl. Will she be okay?"

"She's fine. She's used to this. She's just being a little needy." I play with her soft and fluffy ears as I look at Bente. "We're leaving soon, don't worry."

I take the final bite of the apple pie. It's really good here, although, it could also be the company today. It could definitely also be the company, and the alcohol.

Sanne also finishes her piece and takes the last sip from her glass. "So..." She seems awkward now, and I realise that this would be the moment in a date where we would decide what to do next.

Only, this isn't a date, right? Right?

It definitely feels like one.

A waiter comes over, collecting our plates. "Was everything as you liked it?"

I nod. "Definitely, thank you." I watch Sanne nod, smiling.

"Would you like something else? Coffee? Tea?"

"No, thank you. I'd like the bill please."

"Yes, surely." He goes off and when I look at Sanne she's frowning at me.

"What?"

"I thought we were going to split the bill." She raises her eyebrow at me.

"I'll pay for this. I don't know, maybe you can pay for lunch tomorrow?" Possibly a little bold, but we're both here for the week, and I'd definitely like to see more of her.

"Deal." She smiles. "But you're not getting away from that, you know."

"I know." I grab my wallet as the waiter comes back. "Can you hold her for a moment?" I give Sanne Bente's leash and our hands touch for a moment, shooting sparks through my body. I wish I could touch her more, but this is not the time or place to think about that. Then I follow the waiter so I can pay, and as I return, just seeing Sanne sit there with Bente, all comfortable and happy. It fills my heart.

Bente jumps up as soon as I come close, rushing over, and I grab her, holding her. "Yes, we're leaving now. Just wait a moment longer."

I put on my hat and jacket, and next to me, Sanne does the same. She looks so fancy in her long grey coat, so different from my 'practical' style.

When we get outside, we get to that awkward 'going your own way' thing again. "Where are you staying?"

"Halfway down the Badweg. I'm not exactly sure of the name of the place." She pulls her jacket tighter around her.

"I'm going that way too." I start walking, hoping to stay warm in the icy cold. When we're passing the whale jaws, I smile. "These really haven't changed, have they?"

She looks up too. "No. Same as ever." Then she holds out her hand, a delighted grin spreading over her face.

Then, after a few moments, a snowflake falls on her black gloved hand.

Snow!

Sure, it's cold enough for it, but I didn't expect there to be actual snow. Snow at Christmas is rare, but with just four days until Christmas, here it is anyway. Snow.

I also hold out my hand, watching the flakes fall onto it. Then I look around, more and more flakes coming down.

Not even small ones, but really big ones that probably won't just disappear after a few minutes.

The first snow of the year, and I'm standing here with a beautiful woman from my past at my side. Is it a sign? Is it telling me that I shouldn't be chicken again? That I should take this chance now?

But I know that I'm not brave enough. At least not tonight, not even with more than half a bottle of gluhwein in me. But I've got a week, so maybe I'll get the courage later. Maybe.

Maybe.

3

❄

Sanne

The snow is steadily falling down around us as we walk down the road, back to the warmth of our homes for the week. The white flakes make the world look so different. So much more serene, so much softer. The trees and bushes are all getting covered in a slight layer of white and there is just something about it. It's so beautiful.

Bente keeps trying to catch some of the flakes in her mouth, the dog so excited and happy by the falling snow. It makes the quiet walk back to the apartment easy instead of awkward.

Then the place I'm staying at comes into view, the old building reminiscent of a time long past, a time where this island would have been used for healing people with a range of problems. Though, the actual building isn't that old, but it was still recreated in that same style, some forty years ago.

"This is me." I point at the building. From here I can only see lights in a single other apartment, upstairs on the right side of the house. It seems lonely and empty, just the two apartments filled this week. Although, maybe the people from the other apartments also went out for dinner like I had.

"Really?" Josie grins. "Me too. I'm down at the back of the house."

"I'm at the front." Okay, this is a little awkward now. We're staying at the same place?

"Well, I guess we'll see each other then. Right?" Josie winks. "And you're welcome to drop by whenever you want. Bente and I would love that."

We cross the road, and I don't know what I should do now.

"I'm right at the front here." I point towards the apartment. "You're also totally welcome there."

"Thanks." Josie smiles and then she steps closer. "Hug?"

I wrap my arms around her for a moment and then pet Bente. "You look over her, will you?"

Josie laughs as she starts walking to her own apartment and I watch her walk off for a while before I get to my own apartment.

When I open the door, heat immediately flushes over me. I'm so glad that I turned the heating on before I left, as I've gotten really cold walking back here.

I strip off my warm clothes and look around at everything. I guess I could watch some TV or get some reading done or something. It's not really that late in the evening and I don't feel like going to bed early.

I glance out the window. The snow is still coming down steadily, the big white flakes rushing past the window and slowly covering everything in a layer of white. It's magnificent.

A white Christmas, would we really?

When I wake up, it's chilly in the bedroom. It feels like the heat didn't come on this morning, or, if it did, it may have come on too late.

I glance over to my bag. I've packed some warm clothes, but I don't know if I can get to them without getting cold myself first... I pull the blanket around me tighter as I slide out of bed, pulling it along with me, wrapped around me as much as I can. The floor is freezing cold under my feet and I shiver as I search through my bag. I quickly pull out some thick and warm socks and pull them on. Then I dig through it again to try and find more warm clothes. I take the clothes back to the bed, climbing back in before I put them on, letting them warm up under the covers with me. It's so cold! And the clothes are cold too! Maybe I should stay in a little longer until I'm warm enough to get back out.

I grab my phone from the bedside table and check my email as I warm up. There are some promotional email from webshops, trying to get people to buy some last minute Christmas gifts, which I quickly throw away, and then I go through my social media. There isn't too much going on. My parents are getting ready for Christmas, and they're making some lame 'jokes' about having to spend it on their own instead of with 'family' (aka me). Well, no. I wouldn't have come even if I hadn't been single, but somehow they feel that since I'm back on my own, that I should have been spending it with them instead of going on this trip. I don't know. It's annoying. It's all so annoying. Their ideas that I'd find someone new soon and that I should be looking for a new partner just to spend the holidays with, after being in a relationship for four years, and that somehow I'm pitiful for going on holiday on my own.

Although, knowing that Josie is only a few apartments over, maybe not as alone as I originally thought that I would be. I'd not be against spending more time with her. She's grown into such an interesting woman. And, even though I can recognise her smart tongue from when she was younger, she's also so much levelheaded now, and even more interesting. It's great to listen to her, to watch her tell stories about her practice and to see her love for her job.

I guess she's everything that I'd always wanted to be. Not a vet, I'm not that good with blood and animals who are ill, but her pride and her enjoyment of her job. I'm still in the same job as I was in five years ago. Sure, I've had a few raises, but realistically, I'm still in the same place as I was before. Little has changed. And with everything that has happened in the last months... I feel stuck.

I thought my life was going well, that I was coursing along nicely, but reality is that I'm stuck in the same place that I've been in for a long time, and I really need to get out of here. I need to get moving again. Maybe I can do that this week. Maybe I can finally find my own voice again, my own being, and a new dream for my future.

I look Josie up online. I'd not thought about her in years, and never really considered looking her up. A quick search shows Josie in front of her own clinic, all proud and surrounded by a small team of staff. Everyone looks so happy. I also find some articles about the work she's doing and how much people love her. That all makes me proud for knowing her.

As I keep scrolling down, I realise not just the things that I do see but also the things I'm not seeing. There are some pictures of her with friends and at the clinic on her social media, and of course a lot of pictures of Bente. But there aren't any pictures of a girlfriend or a boyfriend or anything. There is just her in each one of them. Doesn't she have anyone for her at home? A human 'anyone', not just her dog? It almost makes me feel sad for her, although, she seems to be totally enjoy herself anyway. And I guess that also explains Josie coming here so often. She can, because she doesn't have to ask or consider another person, so she does.

That's always been the Josie way anyway. She can, so she does. That's even how we started the whole kissing thing when we were teens. It started as a dare, experimenting, and turned into something that we kept doing every summer, something I looked forward to each summer even though I hadn't really pinned down my whole sexuality yet back then. I was just trying things.

Thinking back makes my cheeks heat up and I think I should get out of bed by now. Hiding under here is making my mind go to places that it maybe shouldn't be going. Remembering things from when we were young. Those days are now behind us. We're grown women, not teenagers anymore.

Right.

I awkwardly get dressed under the blankets, like a little kid, and then slide out of bed. It really is cold. I first go over to the thermostat, it says that it's turned on, but it also shows that it's way too cold here. I shiver as I turn the heat up more, hoping that it will make things a little more comfortable here soon. Then I look around the place, searching for something to eat or drink. I find some tea bags in a cupboard and an electric kettle. That's a start.

I put on some water in the kettle and then open one of the curtains in the living room.

I expected that most of the snow would be gone by now, as it usually is, no matter how cold, but in the early morning light, I'm looking over a thick layer of snow in the front yard and a couple of bird footprints on the snow on the table. It's serene and stunning, like the whole world is quiet.

Someone has been driving a car or bus through the snow on the street, but otherwise, it's almost untouched. I keep staring out the window, somehow feeling calmer now than before. Snow is beautiful. It makes me feel like a kid to just watch the snow on the ground, some parts of it so clean and untouched that it almost looks magical.

I want to go out and walk through it, pick it up in my hands and look at it closely, but I'm also hungry and I need to find something to eat even though I've just woken up.

When the tea has finished brewing, I take my cup and sit on the couch, looking out over the street and the snow, smiling a little. If nothing else, just sitting here in the calm, enjoying the weather, it makes this whole trip worth it.

Then I see someone I recognise come up the road at the side of the building, it's Josie with Bente and she's carrying a bag with what I suspect is food with her. Then Josie glances up to the window and of course catches me looking at her, again. That always happens, she somehow seems to know when I'm looking at her or something. Always. It's unfair.

Then she comes over to the window, holding up the bag. "Do you want breakfast?"

"Really?" Just like that? Out of nowhere?

"I have warm croissants and freshly baked bread." She jerks her head to the side. "Come on over. Take whatever you're drinking now with you." She flashes me a stunning grin and butterflies crash around my empty stomach. Breakfast, with Josie. Yes!

"Okay." I stand up, suddenly not so sure why I'm doing this. I don't want to bother her, and she must have bought it all for herself, and now I'm eating her food. I can't impose on her like that.

A knock on the window makes me jerk and I turn around. "You may want to put on warm boots and a jacket though." Josie is grinning, still standing there, waiting for me.

I pull a face at her as I shake my head. Then I put the tea down and go put on my jacket and shoes. And as I get back to retrieve my tea, Josie is still there. She holds up two thumbs and I can't help smiling at her silliness.

I grab the cup of tea and the keys to this apartment and then get outside, going over to where Josie is waiting for me. "You've got me out of the house, now what?"

"Now it's time for breakfast." She starts walking to one of the apartments at the back of the building.

When I step inside I see that this is very similar in style to the one I'm in. The same colours, though, like my apartment, this one also looks like they've collected different things from different second hand places, as nothing really matches.

But, unlike my apartment, the distinct scent of wet dog greets me. Then Bente rushes past me, immediately going over to the heater and walking in front of it a couple of times, warming up.

I take my shoes and jacket off and then follow Josie to the dining and kitchen area, where she puts the bag on the table and unpacks it.

"I've got croissants, bread, cheese, jam, and all sorts of other things. Take what you want." She grabs some plates from the cupboards and knives from a drawer and puts them on the table. Then she takes a cup of coffee from the coffee maker, she probably made that before she went to get breakfast, and sits down opposite me, smiling at me. "Take something." She nods at the food.

"Pushy." I shake my head, but I still reach out and grab a croissant.

"Nah, you're just slow." She leans back in her chair, her eyes on me making me heat up, it feels so personal, even though I'm fully dressed, I can almost feel her eyes like touches on my skin. "You always used to just wait around instead of diving right in when there was food." Then she sits back up and takes a croissant before taking a small cup with jam. She spreads some jam on the end of the croissant before taking a bite. A blob of jam sticks to her lip and when her tongue darts out to lick it off, I swallow hard.

I need to stop crushing on her. What we did as teens

doesn't mean anything right now anymore. That was then and this is now. I need to stop. I just got out of a relationship and I definitely don't need another one.

Not yet. Even when the woman sitting in front of me makes me all hot and bothered inside. Even then.

Even then.

4

Josie

When I went for a walk this morning, I knew I had to go by the bakery and then the grocery store for food, since I didn't have anything in the apartment yet. And I don't know why, but I couldn't help myself to also get some things for Sanne. It was more a wish than anything, just hoping that I could invite her over.

I felt like such a teenager last night, thinking about Sanne all night. It's been a long time since someone caught my attention like that. It's been much too long...

I watch as she sips from her tea, her movements slow and easy. She looked so surprised when I came walking up the side of the house, and she definitely didn't look ready for a trip into town.

"So." She leans forward a little. "What are your plans for the day?" She takes a bite from her cheese croissant.

"I was thinking of mainly going for walks out to sea and everything. I took a peek just now and the beach looks great, but it was a little too cold to really stay there too long. That, and I was hungry." I smile, shrugging. "What about you?"

She looks out the window, and Bente goes over to her, putting her head on Sanne's lap. Sanne smiles and then pets Bente on her head. "I was thinking of going out to the sea too, but I'm not sure I'm ready to face the cold yet. I didn't expect snow, I haven't packed for snow."

"What do you need? We can probably get it in town."

"Just..." She half-shrugs. "Warm clothes, and maybe boots or something. I didn't pack for slippery snow."

"I can help you with the boots, I think. And for warm clothes, we call that layering, just put more layers on, and you'll be fine."

Sanne grins my way. "You've got it easy, you obviously plan for these things. You're used to them. I don't do cold or snow. I just stay inside the house when that happens."

"And do what?" I'm not averse to staying in either... Especially not when the staying inside is after being almost frozen to the bone looking at the amazing views and ends with spending the rest of the day warming back up with a sexy woman at my side. But that may be a little too forward of me. Maybe.

"I knit, or crochet." Her cheeks flush. "I know, so granny-like."

"No. It's cool. It's totally hot these days. At least, if what the assistants at the clinic are telling me is true. They're talking about those things all the time."

"You don't do it yourself?" Her eyes on me are teasing.

"It's not something that I do. Though, I can, and I don't hate it. But it's not something that I tend to do." I shrug.

"Then what do you do when you're not saving poor pets from procreating and jabbing them with needles to make sure they don't get sick?" She's baiting me now...

"I... ehh..." Should I tell her? She did tell me about her hobbies, but while knitting and crocheting are hot these days... My hobby isn't exactly, still. "I don't really have anything." Oh, that was way too fast, and definitely defensively.

"You don't?" She raises her eyebrow. "That doesn't sound like you. So, you think it's even more embarrassing than granny hobbies, whatever you do? Interesting..." She looks around, but I don't have anything obvious in view. And why would I? I only read digitally, and my ereader is right next to her on the table, all unassuming and plain. No flowery covers to tip anyone off.

"I really don't know anything that I would call a hobby." But I can't help my smile. Dammit.

That makes her eyes sparkle, and she looks around

more seriously now. "You do tricks with Bente and win medals in obscure competitions?"

"Cool. But no."

"You secretly paint bird houses like old Dutch buildings?"

"What? Where did you get that idea?"

"So, you do?" She leans in, hey eyes bright.

"No. Nothing of the kind."

"You..." She looks around again, finally spotting the ereader. "You read hard science fiction books to criticise them on their bad knowledge of science?"

My heart starts beating faster as she picks the ereader up. "That's very specific, and still no."

"Can I look in it?" She points to the ereader.

"S—sure." I swallow hard.

She narrows her eyes at me. "Whatever it is, it's on here, isn't it? Hmm." She unlocks it, and then her eyes go over the titles, her cheeks pinking. "Oh! Romance novels!"

"Yes. Can we drop it now?"

"I'm curious... Just one title." She clicks on something on the screen, and as her eyes go over the lines, her cheeks pink even more.

I have no idea what books she clicked on, but I do know that I was at a very spicy scene earlier today, before I went for a walk.

"'Her fingers slid down the governess' slender waist, to

the curve between her thighs, where she held still for a few moments."' Sanne reads the sentence out loud, and then looks at me. "You read lesbian historical romance novels? *That's* your hobby?"

My face feels like it's on fire as I nod.

"Really sexy ones too?"

I nod again.

"Nice!" Her eyes go over the page again, reading on.

"I was reading that..." I reach out, but she holds it just out of my reach. This is embarrassing.

"I could read it to you, if you'd like me to?" Her eyes sparkle with mischief. "I could read you this really sexy scene between a governess and her..." Her eyes scan the pages.

"Maid." Hey, I've got my favourite tropes, everyone has. But this specifically is one of mine. Although, a good contemporary billionaire lesbian romance definitely gets me going too, I'm not that picky.

"Want me to read it to you?" Sanne's voice lowers a little, and there is a heat in her gaze. "I think this is about to get interesting."

Would I love for her to do it? Sure. But it's not the time right now. "Maybe after a few glasses of wine. I don't think I'm brave enough to listen to you read that to me sober." I swallow hard and stand up to clear the breakfast table off. Giving myself something to do.

"Is that a promise?" I hear Sanne stand up, her voice almost husky, and then her footsteps come closer.

"Maybe?" My own voice is hoarse too.

"You keep making these fun promises, it almost seems like you want me to stay around." Her fingers slide over my back, sending shivers through my body, putting a fire in my core.

"Why wouldn't I?"

"I don't know. You tell me." I can almost feel her body heat at my back, but then she steps away and I hear her pick up the plates from the table and I take a deep breath.

"Do you want to go on a walk later? Check out the beach?" I put the cheese and jam in the fridge and then finally dare to face Sanne again.

She may have teased me about reading sexy books, but she hasn't said anything bad about reading romance novels in general, which is usually what happens when people find out about my hobby. 'Do you read so much because you can't find it in real life?' or 'No wonder you don't have a steady girlfriend, if you think *that's* what real romance is like' or especially the 'a woman with your education, reading *that*?' Like I'm supposed to be reading something else more academically acceptable, just because I have a university degree. That's why I don't tell people. Usually, if my brain isn't totally occupied with a beautiful woman teasing me, I'll tell people I read fantasy (lesbian vampire romance, yes, please) or adventure (lesbian pirate erotica) or, if I'm feeling particularly bold, I'll tell them I read historical books (Regency and Victorian romances tend to be my favourites, those forbidden cross-class romances... Ooh!). But this time, I just didn't know what to answer, not in the least because I was a little distracted by Sanne.

"Do you think I can wear those boots to the beach?" Sanne points at the shoes she'd worn when she came here.

"They look sturdy enough." I clear the final things from the table.

"Do you want to leave now? Or soon?"

I look her over, as she's standing in the middle of the room, her pose a little awkward. "We can leave soon, if you'd like. I really don't have much planned. Walking and reading, mostly."

"Okay." She smiles softly. "I'll..." She nods to herself. "I'll go put on something warmer."

"Do you have leggings or something? You can put those on under your jeans. And maybe an extra pair of socks and an extra shirt." I don't know why I'm telling her all this, she probably knows already.

"You think I'll need that?" Her eyes go a little wider.

"Yeah. It's biting cold out. And there is a lot more wind on the beach. And your feet will start to feel like they're freezing off if you don't wear warm enough socks."

"Of course." She nods. "Makes sense. See? I'm not a winter person."

"But you look so sweet when your face is all red from the cold." I can't help but grin, which makes her whole face flush a deep red. "You go get changed. I'll go finish reading that steamy scene and then we can go check out the beach."

"Yeah. See you soon." And she almost flees from the apartment. I can only smile.

It used to be easy to make her blush, and that's obviously not over. She still goes a great shade of red. I'm mean for teasing her, but I can't help myself when she responds so well.

I should really stop teasing her so much... Especially if I don't want this to get places that I don't know how to quite handle...

After Sanne got changed, she knocked on my door. I put Bente back in her harness and we went out to go the beach.

The street has gotten a lot more flattened since I went for a walk this morning, and even the path on the side of the road has a lot more footsteps going over it now. It's still really cold and the snow doesn't seem to be going anywhere any time soon.

Bente is super excited about the snow still, biting it, running her nose through it whenever she can. It's so funny to watch her. Her excitement about it all. Like she's never seen snow before. She has, she's six years old, but every time she sees it, she turns back into this puppy-like state.

Next to me, Sanne is trying to find a good way to walk on the snow. It keeps getting stuck to the bottoms of her shoes and then she has to stamp it off again every so often.

It's kind of funny to watch, but I do think we may want to go look for something else to wear for her... That's probably a better idea than to just let her struggle on like this for however long this snow is going to last.

She grabs my arm as she's almost falling over, catching me right on time.

"How do you keep doing that?" I laugh as I hold her up. "How can you keep falling over?"

"I'm not used to snow. I don't know how to do this. This is hard, you know?" She shakes her head.

"Just walk at the side of the path, not in the slippery and downtrodden snow, that will probably help some." I help her to my other side, and Bente immediately starts walking right in front of her, really excited about Sanne joining on her side.

"Yes, yes." Sanne laughs as she pets Bente. "You'll help me if I fall, right?"

"Only by licking your face, but you'll have a dog-cleaned face when you do manage to get back up." I grin. "That counts for something, right?"

Sanne looks at me sideways. "Don't listen to her too much, Bente. I know you'll help me."

"Yeah, onto the ground and rolling through the snow." I laugh as I catch Sanne again, this time she nearly got tripped by Bente.

It's fun to have her at my side, and she's definitely not an outside person, not as much as I've become anyway.

No matter how fun she is to talk to, I don't know if it's

a good idea to continue this on after the week is over, especially not when we've really grown up so differently. What's the use when even our hobbies are so different?

Those things just really never work out.

5

Sanne

The walk to the beach is much longer than I remember it to be. Maybe partially because memories always make things seem so much closer by, and partially because slipping and sliding my way forward really isn't the fastest way to move around... And no matter how I keep trying, these shoes definitely aren't the right type for walking in the snow.

As we're finally on top of the dunes, or well, a hill-ish thing that's supposed to be a dune, and where a large hotel is looking out over both the beach and the island, I can finally see the sea.

The grey water and the waves with the white heads on them. It looks almost surreal, not because of the sea, but because of the snow leading up to the sea...

It's almost dystopian. There are a few other people on the beach, but it's probably too cold for most holiday goers and the people living on the island likely don't spend all their time on the beach anyway... So, as far as the eye can see, there are dunes covered in snow and beaches with plants on them, all covered by even more snow, and then, in the distance, there is the dark grey sea.

We walk down the dune, passing a blue building which is labelled restrooms (only open until nine in the evening and during the summer holiday season), rows and rows of beams (bike racks, now totally empty) and some wooden planks advertising activities that only run during the summer months (kiting, painting workshops and beach tours among them), and then we finally walk over the final low dune to step onto the beach.

Josie makes Bente sit down. But Bente keeps looking in all directions, trying to figure out what way to dart off into first, and then Josie finally lets her off the leash. "Don't go too far away." But Bente is already off. I don't know if it's any use for Josie to tell her to stay close, or if it's just something Josie says anyway.

Then Josie stands up straight again, looking at me and smiling. "What do you think? Just listen to it." She closes her eyes, her face towards the wind and she looks so serene, loose strands of her hair flowing behind her, her face still.

But as I copy her, I realise what she's talking about.

46

There are just the sounds of the sea, of the wind making its way through the dunes and the beachgrass and of the snow slightly creaking as the wind blows over it. If I thought the sight was dystopian, this sound is even more so. It's like humanity doesn't exist anymore. Like we're the only ones in this world and there isn't anyone else.

It's kind of creepy, in an 'end of the world' kind of way. But if this is the end of the world, then I don't really mind it if I get to spend it with Josie.

We start walking towards the sea, which is very far away right now, it's probably ebb. First, we walk past a skeleton of beams standing in the middle of the beach, deserted.

"In the summer, they put a bar and things like that on them, but outside of the summer months, it looks like some skeleton of some big creature." Josie also looks at them.

"It doesn't help that the beams are dark like that." I nod. "I bet you can make some great creepy Halloween attraction out of it."

"I bet you can." Josie also looks up at it, a curiosity in her gaze. "Cover it in fabric and then hang things on the inside. I think it can be really creepy." She grins, her eyes shining. "You have the strangest ideas sometimes."

I shrug. "Wasn't that what I was supposed to be, strange?"

When we were young, I was often seen as the strange one. I was quieter, but when I did blurt out something... I don't know, I could say weird things. My brain often went ten places when others were just having a regular conversation, it still does, I just tend to know how to control it better.

Josie picks something up from the beach, a piece of driftwood or something.

Then Bente is suddenly standing right in front of us again, dancing backwards as she keeps her eyes on the piece of wood Josie is holding.

"There you go." She throws the piece and Bente rushes after it, first running way too fast so she slides right over the piece of wood, but then she twists around and grabs it before she brings it back to Josie, all happy. Josie eyes me. "You want to throw next?"

"I'm not that good at that." I frown, but Bente is already standing in front of me, and I take the piece of wood from her. "Okay, I'll try." I hold my arm back and then throw as hard as I can, trying to get Bente to run further this time.

It's so fun to watch her rush after it, so excited just for a piece of wood, and bringing it back and all.

"Do you remember this area?" Josie motions in front of us.

"No?" I look at the beach, but it's all just snow, with some icy-looking bits between them.

"There used to be this trench in the middle of the beach. But they were 'smart' and decided that it would be better to fill it up. And now the water has spread forward more. They used to have a nearly knee deep trench over just a limited area on the beach, but now they have a much larger area with just a little water on it at all times. It doesn't even go away when it's ebb tide."

"Really?" I can't remember that there was a trench in the first place, but having a much larger area covered in a constant layer of water doesn't sound like much of an improvement, at least not when the idea was to probably make more beach available for people to sit on during the summer.

"Yeah." Josie shrugs. "At least we can get to the sea easier now, not having to wade through the water, but with all the snow, I'm pretty sure it would have frozen over anyway."

We start walking again. Bente is running circles around us, the piece of wood still in her mouth, it looks kind of silly.

Looking around, being a little further from the dunes, it's really a spectacular sight.

The sea and the snow together. Things that are from two totally different worlds in my mind, not to exist at the same time, but they still do.

It's magical, in a slightly creepy way.

When we get close to the sea, the wind gets even colder and

I shiver against the biting cold. We're now much further away from the dunes and the wind here comes from over the sea and takes with it small ice particles and the snow it picks up from the beach, throwing it in our faces. There are snow piles as high as my knee that we walk right through and even as I watch it, I can see the snow blowing over the extended beach, constantly moving to new places. It's beautiful, in that 'empty and deserted place' kind of feeling, in a strange way, it feels calming, comforting.

Bente runs at the sea, stepping into it and then rushing out, doing that a few times in a row, pulling up her feet at the cold water.

At my side, Josie lets out a deep sigh. "Bente, please, don't do that, you'll get cold feet and the snow will stick to them." She frowns and she reminds me of a mother scolding her kids, though, I suspect this isn't much different, as Bente isn't listening to her, at all either. The dog keeps running in and out, trying to drink the water a few times.

"Does she always do that?" I look at the dog, almost laughing.

"Yes. She's a silly creature." Josie shakes her head, smiling. Then she looks out over sea. "Don't you think it's so nice and quiet? You can almost hear yourself think here. Unlike back at home."

I shrug a little, not so sure. But then, my thoughts are

always all over the place. "It's more like the wind is blowing the thoughts right out of my head."

Josie raises her eyebrow at me, but doesn't say anything anymore.

We follow the line of the water for a while, simply walking, each with our own thoughts, as Bente goes between trying to get our attention and attacking the sea.

"Sanne?" Josie's voice is suddenly a lot more serious.

"Yeah?" I don't usually like serious questions.

"Do you have pets? You always wanted hundreds of them." Why is that a question that requires a serious tone?

"No. I... Ehh... Never had the time or energy for it. I just..." Is this her roundabout way of asking me about my living situation or something? Pets aren't always a given.

"Not even rabbits? Or a cat?" There is a tone to her voice I don't know how to understand.

I shake my head. "My ex didn't like animals. She was allergic to some of them, so she didn't want any of them in case it got worse. It just never happened to get a pet that wouldn't trigger her allergies." And another reason why I should have seen that the relationship wasn't going to work out way sooner. I still don't know why I was so blindsided by the breakup. And now I'm thinking about all of that while I'm here with Josie, and I don't like it.

"I'm sorry. I shouldn't have pried like that. It's just... You just... I'm sorry." She looks out over the sea again and stops walking. "I guess we both changed as we grew up. And talking about the past as if that's a way to remember who we both used to be... As a way to feel like we still know who the other is... I'm sorry."

I step closer. "Don't be, it's not your fault." I put my hand on her arm, enjoying the closeness. "Of course we changed. It would be strange if we hadn't."

I can't read the emotion in her eyes, but I do know that I don't like seeing it, it looks much too sad.

"Can I ask..." I'm probably on dangerous territory here, but I'm also curious. "Why are you here, on the island? You used to love Christmas with your family." It's somehow one of those details that I do remember about her.

She pulls a face, her eyes hardening. "Like I said, we've both grown up and changed." Then she takes a deep breath. "Let's go back. I'm getting cold." She turns around and I let her go. Surprised by the way she's acting. I asked the wrong question, didn't I?

Maybe she's right. Maybe we've both changed too much. As long as we keep out conversations light and fun, things seem to still match between us so well, but as soon as we get to more serious things... She closes herself away.

Sometimes I see the way she looks at me, that look that whispers of lingering touches and curling up under the covers together. But then she changes and becomes cold, locking me out. I don't know why, but she keeps going between the two.

The walk back feels even colder than the way here. I'm getting much better at staying on my feet though, so I'm not constantly almost falling over. But Josie is quiet and withdrawn, which makes everything seem so much longer.

As we get close to the apartments, I stop. "Hey..." I try to get her to look at me.

"Yeah?" She's not frowning, but that's also not a happy look in her eyes.

"I was supposed to buy you lunch, remember?" I try to flash her my best smile, hoping it will melt some of that coldness around her.

"Oh, yeah." She looks almost surprised. "Maybe dinner? I just want to warm up inside right now."

"Okay." I nod and we cross the street.

Before Josie can walk off, I reach out to her, tugging on her arm so she'll get closer and then I give her a quick kiss on her cold cheek. I step back, a little surprised by my own impulsiveness.

Josie also looks surprised as she stares at me, her mouth slightly open.

"I'll see you later." I try to flash her a smile and then quickly flee to my own apartment, closing the door behind me.

What did I just do? I just wanted her to look happier, but kissing someone out of nowhere is generally not how you do those things. Especially when she looked so serious and I just didn't know what to do...

I know that I used to kiss her all the time and that it would make her happy, but it doesn't mean that more than a decade later, the same thing will still apply. And it's not like I'm in the best position for taking things further anyway...

I've just gotten out of a relationship. Most mornings I wake up and still can't wrap my head around waking up on my own. Or eating dinner on my own. All those things... I'm in no state to even flirt with her, even for a couple of days, but it just feels so good, and it makes me feel warm on the inside...

Why does it have to be so complicated? Things used to be so much simpler when we were young.

6

Josie

I can't believe what just happened. Sanne just kissed me, out of nowhere, after that disastrous walk to the beach.

I tried to make conversation with her, but I'm always too awkward, and when she started talking about her ex not liking pets... It reminded me of the ways in which people change, just to be with someone. It reminded me of the ways people pretend to be okay with things, just because they don't want to be alone.

It reminded me of fake smiles and words that people don't mean. It reminded me too much of fakery.

And I know that I shouldn't have taken it out on her. She was just trying to be nice and answer my question, but to watch her face fall like that... It hurt even though it was ridiculous. I shouldn't feel that attached to her, but I guess that even more than twelve years later, some feelings never go away.

I close the door of the apartment in a daze and take Bente's leash off, letting her roam free. Then I get out of my own jacket and extra clothes.

Now what?

We were supposed to have fun on our walk. But things have gotten complicated and even though I'm good with joking and playing around, that look in her eyes... That didn't speak of joking. And some of the glances she keeps giving me... They're not just joking around either. But then, the pain in her eyes when she thought about her ex. She just got out of a relationship, and I don't want to be the rebound. Nor for her.

I sigh, grabbing my phone and sending a message to one of my best friends, Kara. Kara and I met at some dating event, way back when I was still studying to become a vet and she was studying to become a primary school teacher. We both loved (very cliché) long walks in the forest and along the beach. Only, everything between us has always been totally platonic and we've been walking and hiking buddies ever since. Bente and Kara's dog, Tys, come from the same litter, so we've been having a lot of fun watching them grow up. But apart from that, she's also the one person I trust the most. 'Blast from the past. I ran into a friend from when I used to come here as a girl. And she's still hot.' I smile as I send the message, Kara will understand.

Then I grab my ereader and try to read more of the book, but my mind keeps drifting elsewhere.

My phone buzzes, a message from Kara. 'And single?'

'Yeah. Only recently, though.'

'Oh. Bummer. Still, some wine and candlelight never hurt anyone?' I'm not sure if she's being romantic or oversexed. Then another message comes in. 'I do presume that you like her?'

'I used to more than like her...' Something along the lines of many hot and sweaty nights with myself, since I never dared to even initiate anything more than some kisses with Sanne.

'And now? You said she was hot? That means you have more than just some innocent interest in her.'

'She's heartbroken. I don't want to be the rebound.'

'Sex doesn't have to mean rebound.' Kara is way too practical.

'No. It still doesn't fix anything though. She's three doors down from me, and I'm just sitting here, reading sexy scenes in a book.' I can imagine the look of frustration on Kara's face, she always complains I'm way too reserved when I want things.

'Well, you'll have to figure that out on your own. Either do the girl or woo the girl. But if she shows interest in you, then why not?'

Really, way too practical. 'I'll go read my book now. Talk to you later.'

'Later.' Then she sends a winking smilie after it. Like she didn't just make things more complicated than they already were. I know that when I want things I don't always go about them the right way...

'Do the girl or woo the girl.' Kara's motto. She doesn't seem to have this same problem as I have. Although, I've followed her advise often enough. I've been going on dates and everything, but I never really went further than a couple of dates. I like my freedom too much. I like being able to do what I want to do when I want to do them way too much. And I don't want to bother someone else with some of the more eccentric sides of my personality, like randomly going walking somewhere in the country on a whim.

I don't want to be a bother to anyone, and I don't want others to always have to worry about what plans I'm coming up with now. I don't want them to have to change just to be with me, just to make sense of me or make my life easier.

So, yeah. I've had girlfriends (and some boyfriends), but more than just a couple of dates never really work out for me.

And now I'm feeling down and bummed out again. If my family doesn't badger me with questions of why I haven't settled down yet, my own brain with do it to me anyway. I don't ever get away from it.

There is a soft knocking on the window, and Bente immediately jumps up, barking. When I look up from my book, totally wrapped up in a warm blanket, I see Sanne stand outside the window, looking in, a soft smile on her face. I can't help my own smile, or the little jump my heart makes at seeing her.

I climb out of the blankets and open the door for her. "Hey."

"Hey." She smiles. "I hope I'm not too early."

"Too early for what?" I'm trying to come back to this world, but I've been lost in the world of romance novels a little too long, the hot teasing between the governess and the maid was about to get really good again.

"Dinner?" She raises her eyebrow at me. "It's four in the afternoon."

That would also be why it's getting so dark...

"Already?" I let her in, trying to remember how to 'human'.

"Yes, already." She lets out a laugh and Bente greets her happily. "Have you been reading all day? Aren't you hungry?"

I shrug. "Maybe a little?" She seems to be happier now, not stressed and she's really smiling again.

"Do you want to eat out, or buy some food and I'll cook for you? Or we can even order in, I think. I think I saw something like that when I came in, very modern of them." She walks around the apartment, chatting.

"All options sound good." Now I'm out of my reading induced daze, I realise that I really am hungry and that food would probably be a good option by now.

"You choose. I'm buying." She smiles at me, and the warmth in her eyes make me all gooey inside.

"A combination?" I shrug. "We can walk to the evening store, it's the only place they sell good alcohol around here. And we can order food there, which they will then deliver. Best of both worlds?"

"You've done this before." She grins.

"I have." I put my boots and jacket on, grabbing Bente's leash. When I've put the other end onto Bente, I look up at Sanne. "Is that a plan?"

"That's a plan." She grins. "Sure."

"Good." Kara was right. I don't have to decide anything right away, I could woo her and maybe do her whenever. But for now, I think I'm sticking with woo-ing, for however long that works out.

We leave the apartment and start walking down the road towards the town. Laughing as we slip into the store, ready to get our evening started.

We can take a short detour and let Bente run around

for a while on our way back home, before we sit down for dinner. That way, we won't have to get up until much later in the evening again.

I pour two glasses of dark red wine. This time no gluhwein, like last night, but just regular red wine. I have no idea where from, but it sounded good enough to go with our pizzas. Apparently, our dinner will have a touch of 'grownup' (wine) and a touch of 'can't be bothered to cook' (pizza). We stood in the shop for a long while, trying to decide if we wanted ribs or half a chicken or whatever, until we both settled on pizza instead. Much simpler and easier to choose from, usually.

Bente is already nestled on top of Sanne's feet as I bring the glasses over. The small TV is one of those smart TVs, and I've put on some Christmas movie to watch while we wait. It's not just a combination of 'grownup' and 'can't be bothered to cook' but also a splash of 'sometimes you just want to act like a student, or a teenager' (eating pizza in front of the TV).

But what I love the most is that it's warm and cosy.

We didn't light any candles, the table in front of us is too low and I don't want Bente to accidentally sweep them off with her tail or burn herself on them, and I didn't prepare some fake candles or anything instead.

I sit down next to Sanne, pulling up my feet on the couch, under the blanket we're sharing.

Sanne smiles as she takes a sip of her glass, eyeing the blanket. "Where did you find this? I don't think I've got one in my apartment."

"Brought it from home. It's comfortable." I shrug, then I take a sip of my own glass. The wine is pretty good, for its price anyway.

"Smart." She nods, then she pulls her own feet under the blanket and her toes touch my knee, sending electricity through my body. I don't want her to pull her foot away though, it feels nice, this connection. "How long did they say until the food would arrive?" She checks the time on her phone.

"It should arrive at half past five. So about forty-five minutes left." Which is enough time to start watching a movie and get way too comfortable, and potentially tipsy before it arrives...

"Okay." She hits a button and the movie starts playing, then she slides down more and her whole leg is pushed up against mine, her warmth seeping into me.

I watch her from the corner of my eyes, at the way she intently looks at the screen, the way she smiles slightly, the way she plays with her fingers on the rim of the glass and the way she glances my way, a blush spreading over her cheeks.

"We're supposed to be watching the movie. Not me."

"I know, sorry." I quickly look ahead, my own face heating up a little at being caught, but I also can't help smiling. She was checking on me while I was checking her out.

"I'm not so sure you're sorry." There is a teasing in her voice and I look back at her.

"What?"

One of her hands is no longer playing with the glass, instead hidden under the blanket and I slowly feel her fingertips tease over my knee.

Oh, bold!

"Sanne..." I'm not so sure how good an idea this is.

"What? I'm not doing anything wrong, am I? This is very much pg-13." Her eyes twinkle, and she licks her lips a little.

"Sure. Just..." Then her hand slides lower and her whole hand is on my knee, slowly moving to my thigh. Everything in me tenses in delicious ways, but I grab her hand before he moves further. "Less PG-13 now." I weave my fingers through hers, though I don't move her hand away. Letting stay right there, warm and heavy.

"Like we were PG-13 very often." Her voice is lower now, sexier. "I seem to recall some *interesting* dinners as we were out with friends." She squeezes my thigh a little, and my core echoes it.

"Interesting?" Of course I remember them. Many a hot night was filled with my imaginations of what I'd do if I'd been bold enough to do more, although, it was mostly Sanne who was the bold one when it came to these things, not me.

"I think I remember you liking this." She curves her

fingers a little, raking her nails slightly over the inside of my thigh, and even though I'm wearing jeans, it's like she's touching me right on my skin, making me tighten my muscles in delicious ways.

I close my eyes and then take a quick sip of my wine, trying to hide how much I really want her right now.

"We may have changed in some ways, but you've not changed at all in other ways." It could be interpreted as a complaint or whatever, but when I glance at her, Sanne's eyes are filled with lust. Some things really do not change.

'Do her or woo her.' I'm not so sure that's going to be a decision I'm going to be making myself... It looks like Sanne has already made a choice, and I'm simply going to go along with her.

In more than ten years, I've definitely not changed. Not when it comes to Sanne.

7

❄

Sanne

Sitting here next to Josie is making my head spin in all sorts of ways, but mostly in the ways that I want to make her feel. There are so many different thoughts going through my head, but almost all of them are overshadowed with the knowledge that I'm touching Josie's thigh and that she's holding my hand, not moving it away.

I keep my eyes on the TV, not looking away from it, just focused on it, trying not to stare in the reflection of the window at how Josie's face is getting pinker and pinker or the feeling of how her hand is so hot and heavy on top of mine.

I curl my fingers again, scraping my nails on the inside of her thigh and Josie's hand tightens on mine for a moment. This is so fun, and so heady. I move a little, trying to find a slightly more comfortable way to sit, my arm not at a strange angle anymore.

"Sanne…" Her voice is low, sending electricity through my body. When she gets turned on, the way her voice drops, it's so sexy. Especially when she's trying not to show how I'm affecting her. This give and take, this hide and, well… seeking out pleasure.

"Yes?" I run just my index finger up to her knee a little, and then back down, Josie's breath next to me hitching a moment.

"Nothing."

I can't help my smile, and when I glance at her, her lips are wet and inviting, and I want to lean in for a kiss.

I know that the pizza is going to arrive soon-ish, but it's still going to take a while, and that should be enough time to make her moan out in ecstasy at least a few times, right? I move my hand down a little again, now on the middle of her thigh, before she stops me again.

Still too far to get my fingers anywhere fun…

I put my wine glass down, and Bente looks up at my movements, but then she closes her eyes again, back to her own things. Good.

I turn to Josie, reaching out with my empty hand and I put a loose strand of hair behind her ear.

Her eyes go wider for a moment and then she licks her

lips. "What are you doing?"

"I don't know, what does it look like I'm doing?" I turn as far as I can, my other hand still on her thigh.

"It looks like you're… trying to do *things*." She swallows, licking her lips.

"What kind of *things*?" I carefully take the glass from her hands and then put it to the side, that way we can't spill anything.

"You know… *things*." Her eyes dart away for a moment, before going to my lips as they darken.

"Sexy things?" For all the bravado Josie had in other situations, she's always been a little more reserved when initiating these kind of more sexy and intimate moments.

She nods, her head bobbing up and down fast.

I see my chance as she's distracted, and move my hand a little further down on her thigh.

"Sanne…" She gasps and I take my chance, moving in even closer, putting my other arm around her and making sure I'm close enough to kiss.

"That's my name." I smile. I love having her in my arms like this. I forgot how good she smelled or how just being close to her made me feel all hot inside. My whole body feels like a live wire, energy rushing through me constantly. "I want to kiss you."

Josie's eyes grow again, but then her lips part, just a little. "Yes." It's barely more than a whisper, and the next moment, I close the final distance between us, my lips on hers, her lips on mine.

She's warm, and tastes of wine a little, and soft, and sweet.

Then her, now empty, hand grabs onto my sweater and, as she leans her head back a little, she lets me in more.

I slip my tongue into her mouth, sliding my tongue along hers, teasing her, trying to get her to take some control of the situation too. So good.

Then her other hand lets go of me and both her hands now grab onto my shirt pulling me even closer.

I move my hand up between her legs more, putting pressure on the mound between her thighs through the fabric of her jeans. She moves against my hand, probably not even noticing it, as I deepen the kiss more.

How can she feel so good? How can she make my head spin like this when I'm just touching her?

I slowly kiss down her jaw, a line of nibbles and kisses, as I keep moving my hand between her legs. She's turning into putty in my hands, and the glimpses I catch of her are making my head spin with how sexy she looks.

"Josie," I whisper her name in her ear and she lets out a small gasp.

Then Bente stands up and start barking and we jump apart.

Josie quickly stands up, looking outside, and then going

over to Bente. "There is nothing outside. Why are you barking?" She kneels down next to Bente, not looking my way, but her neck is still red and I hear a tremor in her voice.

The moment is broken now, but I definitely affected her. She was into it and for a moment seemed to have forgotten the things around her. It was beautiful, for as long as it lasted.

"I…" She stands up, looking around, looking a little lost.

"Yes?" I sit back normally and take my glass of wine, my eyes still on her.

"We were watching something." She goes back over to the couch. Sitting down, but this time on top of the blanket instead of under it.

"We were." I look at her sideways, at the way her face is still a little flushed, her breath still heavy. She looks stunning, and just being so close next to her, I know that I want her.

I want her in ways I've not felt in years…

And that pulls me out of my own daze. I just got out of a long relationship, and here I am, about to jump Josie like I'm in heat or something. Like I've not had sex in years…

I'm stupid. I don't need to act like this, I don't want to act like this. Yes, she makes my head spin, but that doesn't mean that I always need to act on those feelings. That doesn't mean that I need to act on them and lead her on or anything…

Downer of the century.

After my small outburst of affection, the waiting for the pizzas gets a little more awkward and I don't know how to break it. So I sip the wine, slowly, since I don't want to get too drunk and watch whatever there is on the TV. It's some Christmas movie, and I know we kind of decided on it together, but I don't really feel like watching it.

"Do you have one at home?" Josie pulls me from my thoughts, suddenly talking again.

"One of what?" I'm lost.

"A Christmas tree." She smiles and then her eyes go back to the TV, before glancing at me awkwardly.

I shake my head a little. "No. I didn't… I didn't really feel in the festive mood enough for one."

She nods, her eyes downcast, but then she looks up again. "I have one at home. Not a real one. And no glass or other breakable decorations on it, because of Bente." She smiles softly. "I put it up early, the lights from the tree always make me feel so welcome when it's dark as I arrive home. It makes the darkness feel a little lighter."

"Ah. Yeah." That makes sense, and I understand the feeling. "I just… I normally have one, just not this year." I shrug. "It's okay. I'm not at home for Christmas anyway."

No real reason to have a tree when I'm not there. It would just stand there, turned off, not being enjoyed by anyone anyway.

Nothing more depressing than that.

"Do you think we can get one here?" She looks at me.

"Here?"

Josie nods, slowly smiling. "Yeah. Just here, or at your apartment, or both. Get some Christmas mood going and such."

"Christmas mood, eh? Like what? Booze? Food? Pretty sure we have those." I look around us.

"Sure. But still, twinkling lights, the scent of pine. Don't you miss that now?"

Twinkling lights and pine make me think of Christmas nights with my ex at home, going over to our families to celebrate, having big dinners, things like that. And I'm no longer going to be doing that, instead I'll be on my own.

I slowly shake my head. No, I don't really miss it, not now, it just makes me feel sad now.

And my strong emotional response to a simple question tells me that I maybe want to lay off the wine, if I don't want to turn into a sobbing mess.

Then Josie's phone rings and she picks up. "Josie here." She listens to the person on the other side of the line and then stands up. "Yes. I'll see you in a moment." She puts her boots on as she looks back at me, and Bente immediately goes over to her. "The pizza is about to be delivered. I'm meeting the woman down the driveway, that way she doesn't have to come all the way up here."

I also stand up. "I'll grab cutlery and such." I bring both our glasses over to the heavy wooden kitchen table and then hunt through the cutlery drawers to find a good sharp knife to cut the pizzas with and forks for eating, though they'll probably not get used anyway.

Good. Food is here. That should distract us for at least a little while. Maybe it can also help me clear my head.

I also grab us both glasses with water. We're going to need some of that if we're not going to get drunk way too fast.

Probably…

Josie relaxes again during dinner, going back to her easy banter and she keeps smiling my way. Was I being too forward, or was the timing just off? I don't know.

I thought we had a fun thing going, but now I'm not so sure anymore. I don't know if I was just imagining things or not, maybe I was too forward… Which wouldn't be the first time, to be honest.

"What's wrong?" I catch Josie's soft gaze on me, she looks worried. "Is the pizza not good?"

I smile at her. "The pizza is great." It's really good,

much better than I expected or am used to.

"Then, what's on your mind?" She's turned into the carer again, trying to take care of me.

"I don't know. I guess I'm just tired." In some ways.

She nods. "Okay. Yeah, I guess." And she goes back to her pizza, although I can still see the frown on her face. She's not going to let this go.

"Are you going to go for a long walk again with Bente, after dinner?" Maybe that's a safer thing to talk about.

"Yeah. I'm going to the beach. Do you want to join us? It's going to be colder than this morning, but the moon should give us enough light to see everything." She smiles a little happier again. "I can even lend you a pair of my boots. Just wear an extra pair of socks and they should fit you."

"That sounds like a better plan. My shoes aren't really up for the snow, are they?"

"Not really." She grins. "The beach is beautiful in the moonlight, and I bet that it looks even better with the snow now."

"Yeah, and I don't want to miss it. You never know how long it will stay." The more I think about it, the better I'm liking the idea.

"Also, very true." She takes another bite of her pizza, licking her lips.

And spending more time outside should definitely stop me from wanting to get too close to her, at least physically.

Maybe that helps the mood too, and if things go bad like this morning, I can always just go back to my own apartment at the end of the walk. Nothing odd about that, right?

I remember the very first time I kissed Josie, and she tried to avoid me for more than a day after it. She's not that good with sudden changes, at least not when it comes to things like this…

Things like being physically or emotionally close to people.

8

Josie

I can't ignore the way my whole body feels all tingly when Sanne looks at me. The way she touched me before... I don't know any other way to describe it than passion, not just lust, but passion, a warmer type of lust.

I thought those kind of situations only ever happened in romance novels, the main character being swept off her feet by a kiss, disoriented by a few touches... If someone would have told me that this would happen to me, I would never have believed them. But now... Now I believe.

Sanne has a much easier time to get to the beach now that she's wearing actual boots instead of the heeled ones she was wearing before.

The moon casts everything in a blue glow, and even

though it's no longer full, it's still bright enough for us to look around, to see the trees against the sky, the snow glistening nearby.

As we walk over the dune and can see the sea, my breath is taken away. The beach and sea under the moon light are always beautiful, but with the snow… It's like a fairytale.

We walk down to the beach and I let Bente off her leash and she rushes off. Probably going to scare some poor pheasant or something, I don't know.

But, as I look around, standing on the beach, it feels different than this morning. There isn't much more but the sounds of the sea, the wind and the snow. And as I look out over sea, I can see the lights of boats and beacons in the distance. It makes it feel a little sinister too.

Fairy tale or nightmare. I don't know. Right now, the two seem to be very close. Very, very close…

Sanne steps closer, and then her hand slides into mine, her grip tentative, but as I tighten my hand around hers, her own grip increases too.

I'm glad I get to experience this with her, because I'm not sure I'll ever see a beach covered in snow like this again, especially not by the beautiful moonlight.

"So different than the full moon during the summer." Her voice is soft and when I look at her, I can see the way she's smiling, then she looks at me. "Right?"

"Yeah." The beach during the summer months,

especially in the moon light, is a whole different thing. "Warm versus cold. And hundreds of voices versus nothing at all." Of course, right then, Bente barks. "Almost nothing."

"Almost nothing." She steps closer. "It's still magical, though."

"Magical or nightmarish?" I glance at her.

"I don't think those have to be different from each other." She squeezes my hand for a moment. "Especially not on nights like tonight." She turns her face to the wind and her hair gets blown back. I can't help but look at her and wish that I could take a picture of her. But that's not really going to be possible, it's much too dark to take pictures.

When I saw the way her face fell as I asked about Christmas trees, it hurt. It hurt to see her feel sad like that. I think I may need to try to get a tree, or maybe at least a few branches for Christmas. And then, maybe, have Christmas dinner together?

Would that be too much?

Would that be sending the wrong signals?

But what are the right signals? I hate seeing Sanne upset, and I want to make her smile. That's all the signal I need to send, all the signal I want to send. But I also know that Sanne may be expecting more from me...

Can I give her more?

As we get back to the apartments, Sanne slows down, looking at me.

"What are you going to do? Are you going to bed yet?" She eyes me.

I shake my head, smiling. "I'm probably going to read for a few hours. I still have to take Bente for a quick trip later in the evening, and I don't want to have to wake up for that." I look over to the apartment. "What are you going to do?"

She shrugs. "I'm probably going to knit a little, maybe listen to music or something like that."

Should I? I don't want today to end yet, but I also don't want to impose on her… "If you want to, you can come knit at my place. And no, that's not an euphemism for anything." I can't help my grin, and Sanne flashes me a grin back.

"I'd like that. I'll just have to grab a few things, but I'll be right over?"

"Okay." I watch as she goes up to her apartment and then take Bente back to my own apartment. Settling her down. She's so cold that she immediately curls up in front of the radiator, on her pillow. Looking at me like she won't leave it any time soon. "We still have to go out later tonight. But you go be nice and warm there for now." I kneel down and pet her a little.

Then I grab my ereader and decide that I should probably read something a little less steamy… Probably, if I want to not sit there with my face as red as a beet as Sanne is simply doing some knitting next to me.

Someone knocks on the window, and when I look up, it's Sanne already, carrying a bag with her.

"It's open." No use locking it when I know she's coming right over. Then I grab my blanket and sit down on the couch with my reader, at a slightly different spot this time, hopefully not too inviting or too much like I do want to do things, or don't want to do things… I don't know.

Sanne takes off the boots and then takes her bag over to the couch too, setting it down at her feet.

I look at the thing she's taking out of it. "What are you making?"

She smiles. "I'm making a sweater. This is the front of it."

"You make your own sweaters? Or is it for someone else?"

"No, this is mine." She tugs on her sweater, the same wool sweater she was wearing last night. "This is also made by me."

"Really?" I reach out, touching it, like I didn't grasp at it a few hours back, trying to hold onto her, not make her stop… But I wasn't really feeling the sweater back then, my mind had been filled with totally different things. "It's really soft."

"I know. It's so nice and warm." She makes herself comfortable on the couch, putting three balls of yarn on the couch next to her. "And I get to choose the quality of the yarn myself when I make things." She grins, a pride and joy shining in her eyes.

"That's nice, and kind of cool." I watch as her fingers and hands move the needles and the yarn in rhythmic ways, not missing a beat.

I keep looking at her for a while before I get back to my book. It's a much tamer romance, a contemporary romance between an author and her beta reader, some second chance type of romance that has all the emotions and feelings, exactly what I like. But from time to time, I can't help but glance up at the almost machine-like way Sanne is moving her hands, totally getting engrossed in what she's doing and the concentration on her face is too sweet not to keep watching.

Then she glances at me, smiling a little. "Do you want me to make you one too?"

"What? Me? Eh… I don't think that's a good idea. That'll take months to finish." I stammer, not sure what to say. Too surprised.

She grins, shrugging. "It'll surely be done before next Christmas, I'm pretty sure of that."

I can't help smiling myself. "Even then."

Sanne looks out the window, her eyes going wistful. "It would make a great excuse to see you again, you know?" Then she glances my way. "More than just once in a decade."

"Oh." I quickly look away, before I look back at her. I hadn't thought about that part of it.

Kitting a sweater takes months, probably. And she'd probably need to take my measurements, make me try it on… That's multiple times of meeting up and seeing each other.

"Maybe?" My voice barely comes out. "If you… If you'd really like to…"

"I offered, didn't I?" Her eyes twinkle.

I nod. "Yeah. Thanks." My cheeks heat up and I quickly look back to my book, trying to read the page again, trying not to get too distracted.

It's quiet, the only sounds the clicking of Sanne's knitting needles and the light snoring from Bente.

Even though it's a little awkward, it's also nice. Not being alone, but also just being able to do our own thing without having to worry about what the other one is doing.

I glance up at Sanne for a moment, she really seems like she's enjoying herself, like she's used to just sit together and doing her own thing and doesn't want to do anything in the world more than to just be together. It calms me down more. Maybe everything is okay, maybe we can do our own thing when we're together.

Maybe… But one night of things going over easily doesn't really say anything. I know that all too well.

When we reach Sanne's apartment on our way back from walking Bente for her final trip, we stop. She's rubbing her hands together and looks ready to go to sleep.

"I guess this is where I drop you off?" I look at her, wondering if she'd kiss me again, and if I'd be disappointed if she didn't…

"Yes. I guess it is." She smiles, but it's an exhausted smile. "I guess I'll see you in the morning."

"Want me to make you breakfast again?" I liked it, seeing her so early in the morning.

"I'd like that." She nods. "That had been a really nice surprise to wake up to."

"I'm happy to please." I look her over. "You should probably go get yourself somewhere warm."

She nods again, grinning. "I guess this is where our night ends?"

"I guess it is."

"Goodnight." She leans in, and I give her a quick kiss on her lips.

"Goodnight." I take a step back, my heart already

beating fast again.

"See you in the morning." She smiles as she gives me a small wave and then goes into her apartment, disappearing from sight and I let out a deep breath. That was… Yeah.

Today was definitely a day to remember.

I go to my own apartment, closing the door, and then lean back against it, closing my eyes. Spending the day with Sanne was scary and amazing, and has definitely made me feel more alive than I have in months. But that doesn't mean that this will be more than a holiday fling, a Christmas fling…

I turn the lights off behind me and take my ereader to my bedroom. I undress and get into bed, the sheets are still cold, but they'll be warmed up soon enough. Then I take my ereader and open a steamy erotica book, clicking through it until I reach the part that I want to read.

Then, as my eyes go over the words, I let my hand slide down under the covers, tracing my stomach until I reach the lacy fabric of my thong. I let my fingers slide further, over the fabric, the sensation of the fabric against my most sensitive parts exciting.

Then I put the reader aside and close my eyes instead. Remembering how Sanne touched me. Her fingers not even on my skin and still turning me on so much. Her movements, her kisses, the way she rubbed all my sensitive places…

The way she said my name…

The way her kisses made me lose my mind…

The things she could have done, the things she could have done to me, if Bente hadn't barked, the things that the Sanne in my dreams did more than a decade ago, the things she does in my dreams now.

Things that I'm way too insecure to initiate, but which she always seems to know that I enjoy anyway…

Sanne…

9

Sanne

When I wake up, it's definitely earlier than it was yesterday. It's still a little dark outside and the gap between the curtains lets in a grey light.

I curl a little deeper under the covers, at least the bedroom isn't almost freezing cold when I wake up, like it was yesterday, it's a pretty nice temperature now. But that doesn't mean that I want to get out of bed yet.

I check my phone, but there isn't much on social media or in my email inbox. Which is good, on the holiday side of things, but it also feels a little lonely. Maybe I should get Josie's numbers today… I totally forgot about that before, but it would make meeting up a lot easier. Especially after this is all over… Especially when we're going back home again…

Okay. Time to get out.

I throw the covers off and grab a towel. Then I put together today's outfit and take that with me too, I spotted a radiator in the bathroom, this way I won't have to leave the warmth of the bathroom to put on warm clothes. I do know that it's a little childish, but nobody can see me, I'm here all on my own, so I can do whatever I want.

That makes me stop for a moment, considering that thought. I'm on my own, I can do whatever I want. And I'm okay with it.

For the first time in months, I'm okay with being alone. The empty apartment doesn't feel lonely, it feels freeing to have all this space, and to have all this space to myself.

I smile as I step into the bathroom, quickly putting the towel and the clothes over the radiator and turning on the shower. As the space steams up, I quickly brush my hair, and then feel if the shower is hot enough. Definitely!

I turn the temperature down a little and step into the shower, letting the water fall over me, letting everything steam up and fill my head with that instead of thoughts. Just being in the moment.

As I wash my hair, I rub my skull and for a moment, I imagine Josie doing it. No, I don't imagine. I remember. I remember us taking a shower together at the end of the day, washing each other's bodies and each other's hair after a day at the beach… Her fingers in my hair, rubbing my skull, it would always make my legs weak and almost make me lose focus as she really dug in, releasing all the stress. I try to do it on my own, but I'm not sure if it's just the angle at which I'm doing it, or if it's because it's not Josie, but it's not the same.

I quickly rinse the shampoo out, and as I let the conditioner do its job, I brush my teeth. I should probably not dawdle too long, especially not if I want to catch Josie before she goes on her walk with Bente. Going to the stores together for breakfast sounds like a great and fun plan, especially if this eating breakfast together thing is going to be a common occurrence for us when we're here.

I would like it to be. For all my thoughts of feeling free when I'm in here by myself, spending time with Josie is giving me different feelings, which are just as good, or maybe even better.

Maybe even better…

As I get out of the shower, my hair still in a towel, I catch Josie and Bente walking through the path next to the house. I quickly go over to the window and knock on it, trying to get their attention.

I feel a little silly, knocking this hard. But it works and Josie comes over to the window, grinning.

"You're not coming all wet like that. You'll get cold." She points to my hair.

"I'd hoped to come." I pull a face. She's right, if I go with wet hair, I'm bound to get a cold and that's no fun on holiday, or ever really.

"I've got a better idea. You dry up, and in about twenty minutes, we'll walk by again and then you can come join us for breakfast and we can go for another walk after. Is that a better plan?" She grins.

"Probably." I nod. "Fine. I'll see you in a moment."

"See you in a moment." She gives me a small wave as she walks away from the window again, passing in front of the apartment and waving more there, grinning, and I'm pretty sure I'm also grinning at her.

When they're out of view I don't know what to do immediately. I could probably make tea again, but I can also do that at Josie's place later, or get some coffee there…

So, instead, I grab my bag with my knitting projects and look through it, this can keep me busy for a while.

When I'd offered Josie to make her a sweater too, I wasn't very serious, but the way she responded was much too sweet and I do like the idea of making her something, even if just to know that she's wearing something I made, or to meet her again…

I dig through my bag, trying to find out if I still have my leftovers in here and find a set of double pointed needles and a dark red, almost wine coloured, yarn which I'd used for some details on a different project. If I can't make her a sweater yet, I can make her a hat instead, and that could be an interesting Christmas gift too. Not too fancy and fairly fast to knit up. Sounds like a great idea.

I'm all into my own world of knitting and purling in the right order when there is knocking on the window and Josie is standing in front of it, waving at me, grinning. "You coming over for breakfast?"

"Sure." I put my knitting project away and then put my shoes and my jacket on.

When I open the door, Josie is still waiting for me at the window, her nose and cheeks all red as her eyes sparkle.

"Cold walk?"

Josie rolls her eyes as she lets out a laugh. "Nah, it's boiling hot out here."

I reach out, putting my warm hands on her cheeks, feeling how cold they are. I do it on a whim, but when I meet Josie's eyes, the feelings in them make that I don't pull away, not yet. "They're really cold." I clear my throat, my voice a little odd.

"Then why did you ask?" Josie's voice also dropped a little, and then her arm slides around my waist, pulling me closer. "Do you want to feel how cold my lips are?" She's grinning, but there is also an uncertainty in her eyes.

"Let's see." I lean closer, and as our lips touch, they

really are really cold. But more than that, Josie's arms around me tighten a little and then her tongue teases against my lips, trying to get me to let her in, and as I do, our tongues slide together. Electricity shoots through my body, setting everything on fire and making me want more, even this early in the morning. It's like I don't even know what to do anymore...

When Josie pulls back, her eyes are dark and she's got that slow happy smile on her lips.

"That was cold, but not for long." I grin.

"Well, if it's cold, we need to warm you up." She starts walking, pulling me with her to her apartment. She seems a lot more confident today, although, I never know how long that lasts with Josie, she can be a little unpredictable, but that's mostly her insecurity, which I've always known.

At Josie's apartment, we quickly strip off our warm clothes, the apartment a nice toasty temperature anyway, and Josie has already set the table.

"You didn't have to." I stare at the table, it looks a lot more fancy today, everything spread out nicely and there is even orange juice. "When did you get all this?"

"Yesterday." She grins, going over to the coffee maker and getting herself a cup. "I just didn't put everything on the table." Then she looks at me. "Coffee or tea? And would you like a boiled egg?"

"Tea, please. And ehhh… an egg?"

"Yeah." She turns on the electric kettle. "I've got eggs. If you want to. I'm making some for myself anyway." She takes a box of eggs from the fridge.

"Yeah. Thanks. I'd love some." I sit down and Bente is at my feet immediately, wanting a lot of hugs and cuddles. She's so soft and sweet, and I love just running my fingers through her fur.

Then Josie puts a cup of tea on the table in front of me. "Don't spoil her too much, or I'll have to put up with her begging for months." But as I look up at Josie, she's grinning broadly.

"Oh, how horrible." I grin back. "I'd bet that if I came by a few times a month, that she'd be fine. Right, Bente?" I ruffle the fur on her head and she pushes her nose against me.

"Well, if you put it that way. I'll hold you to that." Josie's eyes on me are heavy and I swallow hard. That look speaks of something much less innocent than just coming by to pet her dog… It speaks of a very different kind of *petting*.

"Maybe." I pet Bente absentmindedly, feeling my body heat up again.

After the kiss and touching last night, I keep wanting to do things to Josie, with her, but I don't know if it's even a good idea to go there…

After breakfast, we curl up on the couch, this time watching something a little more interesting than last night and I don't know, I don't mind this. I like curling up with her like this, it's comfortable and warm and nice. It's cosy.

"Do you remember that summer when they were redoing part of the hotel and we'd sneak behind the building things and get into the redecorated rooms?" Josie laughs.

"I think we may have stolen a lamp or something from one of the rooms?" I try to remember, but I mostly just remember Josie and her irresistible laugh as we'd slip behind the plastic screens, away from the prying eyes of other people.

"A lamp?" Josie snorts, her eyes shining. "Not a lamp."

"What?" I blink. "I thought it was a flashlight or something. I know you grabbed it."

"Fleshlight maybe, but no. It was a vibrator."

"What?" I sit up more, looking down at Josie.

"You really didn't know?" She grins as she looks up at me. "For someone so over sexed, you were very innocent too, you know? Yeah, you heard me, vibrator."

I stare at her, my mouth open, until I remember to close it. "Why didn't you say anything?" Then I remember the thing she's talking about. The day we sneaked in and found out that someone else had probably had the same thought the night before, having left a few items behind. A beach towel, some condom wrappers and I also remember a fairly big black *thing*, which I'd presumed was a flashlight, mostly because of the size. "*That* was a vibrator?"

Josie closes her eyes as she nods. "Yeah. That was a vibrator. Batteries weren't even dead."

"What?! You used it?"

"No." Her eyes go wide as she shakes her head. "But I did turn it on to test it before throwing it away. I didn't want it, I was just... surprised someone would leave it behind."

"Maybe the person had better things to focus on when they forgot to take it back with them." Like a very sexy person to have fun with instead.

I admit, I was pretty innocent in anything but the most basic of 'sex' things. I knew what kissing and heavy petting was like, and yeah, I'd had sex with guys, and I was definitely experimenting with Josie. But I didn't really know anything outside of that. I had no idea about sex toys or things like that, none.

I was pretty innocent. And very naive.

But it also made so many things so much more fun, like locking myself in the bathroom with Josie during a party, and getting so hot from kissing that we'd grind all up to each other.

Those first things, those first things with a woman. They've all been with Josie, Josie was my first in many ways. And even now, just being near her sets my body on fire...

Like the last twelve years never happened. Like we're

still eighteen and don't have a list as long as our arm of disappointed experiences each…

Like we haven't changed at all…

10

Josie

Curling up on the couch with Sanne is so much fun. It's still really cold outside, but it's warm and cosy inside, especially right here. It also reminds me so much of the summers we used to spend together, all the hours and days and weeks we'd be here and get into trouble together and everything, before we'd just sort of crash together at the end of the day, relaxing instead.

Sometimes I ache when I remember those days and wonder where the brave version of me went. I wonder when I started to become so much more… cautious and less brave. I was the wild one of us, at least when it came to getting into trouble, or the way I dressed (though that could totally have been overcompensating for being pretty shy, by the way).

These days, I mostly spend my time working at the clinic, reading books or walking with Bente, and not much else. No more crazy antics, no more doing weird and silly things. I don't know, being here with Sanne reminds me of all I used to be and makes me wish that I didn't feel so boring now.

Sanne moves a little, pulling me a closer. "You're comfy and warm." Her breath is so close to my neck, it makes my body respond instantly.

"Yeah?" I try to look at her, but I can't move my neck that far back. "And why does that have to be mentioned right now?"

"Because I like it." I can hear the smile in her voice, the way she's relaxed.

"I don't think I would have expected anything else from you." I can't help my own smile. What's up with her and being all gooey?

"True. It's just…" I feel her shrug, her body moving against my back. "I haven't cuddled up with anyone like this in a long time. I forgot how good it felt." There is now a tinge of sadness in her voice and I feel sad too. Nobody should feel like they're missing out on something as simple as hugs and cuddles.

"Hugging feels good and warm, usually." I lean back against her more, before I look to the side. "You can also hug Bente, if you'd like to."

Bente looks up as she hears her name, her eyes filled with interest, but as she sees us not moving, she puts her head down again. We're no fun to her if we're not moving, that, or don't have food with us.

"I don't think I can do *this* with Bente." I feel Sanne's breath on my neck again, her soft and warm lips following soon after, leaving behind kisses, making my heart beat faster.

"No, I don't think so." I hear how my voice has changed a little, got rougher. "I think that would end up with you having a lot of hair in your mouth."

"Yeah, probably." Sanne lets out a bright laugh. "A mouth full of a lot of black and white hair, I presume." Her whole body moves slightly as she laughs, I can feel it against mine. I like listening to her laugh, I like making her laugh. I like all of that.

I may be liking it a little bit too much… A little too too much. But right now, that's good. Right here, that's good.

We're in the middle of watching an episode of some American crime series, when my phone rings. It's the ringtone for one of my assistants, Eline. That's not good, she wouldn't call me unless there was something wrong.

I quickly get up and get my phone from my bag. "Josie

here."

Bente also stands up, pushing against my legs as I look out the window, surprised by my sudden movements.

"Hey. Sorry to disturb you, I know you're on holiday and that you really needed the break and everything. But..." Eline doesn't sound very happy, and she rambles when she's nervous.

"Yes?"

"I just got a call from Loes' husband that she made a bad fall this morning and they're at the hospital right now. It seems that Loes has broken her arm in two locations and she won't be able to cover for you this week." Eline lets out a deep sigh.

That's definitely not good. "Is she okay, otherwise?" I share my clinic with Loes, she works one day in the week and takes the emergency calls over the weekend, which lets me spend some time on other things too.

Why didn't her husband call me instead? Well, I kind of know why... I'm supposed to be on holiday and not returning any time soon...

"Yeah. He said that she slipped when she was walking down the driveway and caught herself wrong and hit something on the way down, apparently a bad fall, but she got of lightly with just her arm. Loes seemed fine otherwise, just that she couldn't work for now." Eline sighs. "I know that you're away, but I just didn't know what else to do, who else to call. It's your place, and I know that she was supposed to take over for you this week."

"Yeah. Thanks." I'm already running the times of the ferry through my head. I should be able to get home today so that the clinic can open like normal tomorrow. I'll still need to pack and clean here, and then get to the boat... I should be able to get home, probably... "I'm coming home immediately."

"No. You don't have to. I can call around, see if someone else can help out. Don't just come back, not yet. We'll make it work." I know that Eline is trying to keep me on holiday, since she was the one insisting I should take some time off.

"No. It's my place. I'll come back home. Everyone in the county is going to be understaffed in the coming days, and you know what happens on holidays. Loads of people not paying attention to what their pets sneak from tables and with this snow..." I look back to the couch and find Sanne look at me with a worried gaze. Leaving will mean leaving her behind here... "I'm going to pack and clean up this place and I'll come home. I'll cover for myself. See you in the morning."

"See you in the morning. Sorry to break up your holiday."

"It can't be helped. See you tomorrow." I disconnect the call and then put my phone on the table. Fuck. So not part of the plan.

"You're leaving?" Sanne stands up, her eyes sad.

"Yeah. The vet who was supposed to take over for me for the week broke her arm pretty badly, and I just have to go back." I don't want to leave her behind, but this is my clinic, this is my job, and I can't not be there for them... "I'm sorry." My heart is heavy but Sanne wraps her arms around me.

"It's okay. I get it." She's soft and warm as I wrap my arms around her too, holding her close. I don't want to have to let her go.

"I'm still sorry. I wish it was different."

"I know you do." Her voice is soft. "But you have to do this. I get it. It's your clinic." She keeps holding me for a while longer and I ravel in her closeness, in her scent and her touch.

Then I pull back, strengthening myself for the hours ahead. "I need to pack and leave this place clean." I sigh, looking around.

Sanne smiles at me encouragingly. "I'll help. Two is faster than one."

I eye the kitchen. "You can have the food from the fridge and everything. I'm not taking it home with me. And I don't think you've got anything at your place right now." When I look at her sideways, she nods, grinning awkwardly.

"Yeah. Thanks." Then she sighs too. "I guess we should

probably start?"

"Yeah." I nod, not feeling up for it.

Bente already feels something is going on and she keeps walking right in front of us, almost tripping us, trying to make sure that we won't leave her behind.

"I'll do the bedroom, you start at the kitchen?" I linger my fingers on Sanne's hand and she takes them for a moment before she nods.

I wish I didn't have to leave, I haven't even been able to do any of the things I wanted to do with Sanne this week. Like make her a lovely dinner, or make love to her...

It seems like this is another chance missed. Another chance that didn't happen.

Another one of those mistakes I'll forever wonder about...

I step out of the apartment, turning off the last lights, as I'm carrying one bag and Sanne is carrying two more of them, Bente pulling on her leash as she keeps looking around. It's already starting to get dark, even though it's just four in the afternoon, it makes it feel so much later.

We carry the bags to the bus stop in front of the apartments, at least we don't have to go very far with them. But that doesn't make it any less sad or annoying for this to happen.

When we're at the bus stop, Sanne turns to me, looking

me over. "Well, it was fun seeing you for a couple of days." She tries to smile, but I can see the sadness in her eyes.

"Yeah, it was fun. We should definitely meet up more often. Especially since we don't actually live that far apart." And I really should make time for her, just because she always makes me feel happy when I'm with her.

"We should. At least we can now send messages and everything." She smiles more now, stepping closer. "I hope that everything at the clinic will be okay, and that your colleague is feeling better soon."

"Thanks." I smile back. "And you have a couple more days of holiday here. Make them the best they can be." I take her hands, then I lean in and her lips are on mine.

A final kiss, before we're going to be apart for I don't know how long. It can be weeks, months or years, again.

Well, I'll try not to make it years, but I have no idea if it's going to be months or weeks... I never seem to know these things. I suck at having a good work-life balance, especially for the things I like the most, or the people I like the most.

Sanne wraps her arms around my waist, pulling me closer. "Stop thinking, just be here right now." She's still smiling, but I also hear the worry in her voice. "We'll talk soon, and we'll see what happens from there. Yeah?"

I nod, before she gives me another hard kiss and the lights from the bus to the ferry fall over us.

My heart is heavy as I step back. "I've got to go."

"I know." She nods, grabbing two of my bags, holding

them again, and I take my tickets, one for me and one for Bente.

As the bus stops, Bente jumps in and I follow her. "Talk to you soon." I wave at her as the bus driver stamps my tickets, and then I take the bags from Sanne.

"Talk to you soon." Sanne waves as the doors close, and then takes a step back, wrapping her arms around herself in the icy cold.

I walk further into the bus, it's almost fully empty, which doesn't surprise me. When I sit down, I spot Sanne still standing at the side of the road and I wave at her, before she waves back at me with a sad smile.

The bus drives off and I lose her out of my sight. I sigh deep. I don't like this heavy feeling in my chest, but I also know that this wasn't really a choice I could have made any differently. My clinic needs me, that has to go first.

Let's hope we get to see each other again soon, that's all I really want.

I'm glad I got to spend a couple of days with Sanne before I had to get back to my normal life, but it's not different from what it was before. I chose this life, owning my own clinic, and I knew that it would mean full dedication from me, and trying to have whole weeks off from it just wasn't really something that was going to work out anyway...

I'm not in a place to start anything more than a couple of hookups with people, or keep sort-of friends. I'm not in a place to have relationships of the partner type, not now anyway... Not now I'm still building this clinic, which will probably take even more years to come... I should have known this wasn't going to work out.

I look over the fields as the bus passes them, all covered in a thick layer of snow. It looks so serene, it looks like a real fairytale type of Christmas scene. I've had some days to myself, and now they're over again. That's life.

These last days were like a dream and now I have to get back to reality. Reality and a combination of memories and imaginations of what could have been with Sanne. Well, that, and romance novels, since those are apparently the only type of relationships I can really keep, me and my books...

When we drive onto the pier to the ferry, the mudflats stretching out in front of us are a curious sight. They're also covered in ice and I can see even more snow here. It still feels unreal to see the combination. But I guess, like every once-in-a-lifetime experience, this weekend was something I'll only ever be able to experience again in my memories...

11

Sanne

My heart is heavy as I get back into my own apartment. It's a little chilly here and I already miss having Josie around. She was so soft and warm and just being near her made everything feel better.

I understand that she had to go. It's her clinic, she had to go back. That's what people with their own companies do, at least the ones who actually work at their own company in any real capacity. Rationally, I know this, but it still makes me feel childish that I just wished that she didn't have to go, that I wished she'd just call someone else to cover for her or whatever. I feel selfish for those thoughts, for wanting her with me here longer, but this is reality, not a fantasy.

I sit down on the couch and turn the TV on, putting something random as background sounds as I grab my knitting bag. I just don't know what to do now, how to entertain myself, nothing feels fun anymore. Like I've somehow lost the ability to entertain myself, just by being near Josie for a couple of days.

Sighing, I switch to another program, trying to find anything that gets my attention more than basically me wanting to turn it back off, but the silence is also too overwhelming. When I've found some TV drama, I go through my knitting bag and find Josie's hat. I could still finish it, and then give it to her next time I see her. If it can't be a Christmas gift, at least I can finish it for the next time I see her. And maybe, just maybe, I can imagine I'm not totally on my own here.

Alone in this apartment, alone on this island.

What was I thinking before? How did I think this was going to work out? Me? Here? Alone? I'm just so stupid sometimes.

I start the knitting, my hands doing the stitches automatically, putting me almost in a sort-of trance like state as I try to keep distracting myself. And, finally, after a while, it seems to work.

I'm finally able to just be. Just do my thing.

Even though there is this constant voice at the back of my head telling me that I let yet another chance slip...

Dinner on my own is boring. It seems Josie had planned on pasta with steak and some sauce, all the ingredients were already there. And it did taste pretty nice, although, I'm sure that Josie is a much better cook than I am.

I'm eating in front of the TV, since sitting at the table on my own just feels pathetic right now.

As I'm about to take another bite, my phone buzzes with a message, and as I pick it up, I find it's from Josie.

'Got home safe. There is even snow here everywhere.' She's attacked a photo of a long driveway and fields with snow on them, and of course, Bente is in the picture too, a black and white streak as she's running around.

I can't help my smile, my heart fluttering a little. 'Looks good. And glad to hear you've arrived safely.' Then I send another message. 'What did you have for dinner? Or what are you having for dinner?'

Josie doesn't reply immediately, probably getting her things into the house and everything, so I put my phone down, looking at the program on the TV again, taking a couple of bites. Then I get a reply, just a picture of a deep fryer on top of a freezer or something, it doesn't look half as good as what I'm having.

'Fries?' Likely.

'Whatever I have in the house, I have no idea yet. I hadn't planned on coming back late on a Sunday, so there are no stores open right now. But I know that you've got a good dinner, probably?'

I smile. 'Yeah. Thanks. I made the pasta and the steak, it tasted really nice.'

'Good. Glad to know at least one of us is enjoying it.' Then she sends a laughing smiley.

I don't know what else to send her, what to tell her or ask her. Being apart feels weird now, feels strange. So I don't send anything and instead finish my dinner.

Josie doesn't send another message either, so I leave it be. No matter how much I wished I could talk to her, hear her voice. I'm scared that if I call her now, I'm going to cry.

I don't know why, but just being alone is hurting now. Knowing that this morning I was still cuddling with an amazing woman, and now I'm on my own again. It just brings back so many bad and dark feelings from the past months. It's silly, but it feels like my heart got broken all over again and as the feelings of what it was like to hold Josie, of being held by her, flow through me, tears start pricking at my eyes.

I don't want to cry. I don't want to cry all over again, but I don't know how to stop it. I don't know how to make the tears stop.

Being alone wouldn't hurt this much if it wasn't part of being left alone. Being left here, on my own, with nobody around. Again...

I wipe the tears away with my sleeve, but it doesn't help. They just keep coming, my chest hurting, and I wrap my arms around myself tightly.

I wish Josie was here with me right now. I wish I could hold her. I wish that she could hold me. It shouldn't hurt so intensely, but it does.

It always hurts, it has always hurt.

Sitting here, staring into nothingness, with tears sliding down my cheeks makes me remember the nights I would feel so alone when the summer was over. Usually, Josie had to leave first, always having to do things before the new school year started. So, while she was gone, I would still be on the island, always feeling so lost.

When we were here, it was always *us*. *We* went places. *We* did things. This island was *our* place. And to be here without her, it felt like I was missing half of myself. I always felt so lost when she'd already left while I was still here.

It's stupid that I didn't realise at that age why I felt so strongly. Why being here without her always upset me so much. Why I just didn't feel the same without her. I was naive and silly, unknowing.

I've always loved her. Her laugh. The way she would grin and tease me. The way our eyes would meet across the room and she'd flash me that sexy smile, knowing that we'd be sneaking off together soon. All of that.

The very first moment I saw her, the defiant look in her

eyes, the way she was standing, her head up high... It made my heart beat a little faster and immediately made me smile.

Being around her made me happy, pure and simple.

I've always loved her, even if we didn't name it like that back then. We called it 'having fun', we were 'summer-best friends'. We were 'summer twins', two people, one mind. One heart.

I don't know if it felt like that for her too, that need to always be together. That need to always do things together. I thought that we both did, but this was before social media was the place to be, the place to connect with everyone. This was before looking someone up on social media to find out if they had a boyfriend or girlfriend before you went on a date with them. This was before all that.

I lost Josie once. I had no idea what this feeling I had for her was meant to be, I had no idea, and I've already lost her once.

I'm not losing her again. I'm going to keep in touch with her, we're going to keep meeting up. I'm not losing her again.

Not now.

As I wake up, my eyes are still a little rough and my head feels heavy. I cried way more than I thought I would. Somehow, I just felt so crappy and that overtook my whole evening until I went to bed. At that point, Josie had already left for bed, she'd sent me a sweet message right before she did, and of course, that had set off the whole lonely feeling with the tears again...

I sit up, blearily looking around. A calmness has settled over me during the night, a calmness and determination.

I'm not going to wallow, I'm not going to sit around and not do anything. I've been doing that way too much, and it's time that ends.

I get out of bed, immediately getting dressed, before I check my phone.

There is a simple message from Josie. 'Getting ready to open the clinic. It's stunning outside.' Attached is a picture of the same driveway I saw before, now snowed over again, no tracks left from last night. Although, I think I can see some footprints from Bente in it. The picture was sent an hour ago and I send her a reply.

'Just got out of bed.' Then I open the curtains and take a quick snap of the snow in front of the apartment before I send it to her.

Josie has probably already started her work, it's nine in the morning. At least I slept in, that's good, somewhat.

I make myself some tea and some sandwiches and then sit at the table, checking my social media and email. Although, I don't really find anything interesting there. I leave some replies on cute Christmas pictures from my parents and some people from work, and then cyber-stalk Josie for a few moments. She's really not that into social media, apparently. I don't find more than I had before, and upon further inspection, most of those pictures weren't posted by her but by people who tagged her in the pictures. She's pretty quiet online. Which makes me smile. I hadn't expected that exactly, she was always so outgoing, but it's interesting to see.

Then I put the phone away again, finishing up my tea and deciding on the next thing. I should probably go take a walk on the beach.

I came here for the island, the beach, and I'm going to do that. I'm going to take some more pictures of there and then take a long walk. Enjoy the island as I had planned on. And then, at the end of the day, I'm going to put into place the next part of my plan.

First, the island.

Then, I'm going home and make this Christmas worth every bit of anticipation I had these last days. I was really looking forward to spending it with Josie, even if the plan formed in just a few days, and if she has to work most of Christmas day, I can still make it a good Christmas for the both of us.

We don't have to both spend it alone, better yet, neither of us has to spend it alone.

While Josie is working and taking care of others, I'm

going to make this a great Christmas, just for her, for us. Josie is amazing and makes my heart flutter, and I don't want to lose that feeling this Christmas. Just, no. Not going to happen. I'm going to make this Christmas the best and most intimate Christmas she's ever had.

If she hadn't planned on celebrating Christmas at home, and she has to work all day, she probably doesn't have anything in the house and probably doesn't have the time to go shopping or prepare delicious food herself. I can do it for her and surprise her with it.

Just thinking about that makes me feel better, gives me energy again.

First, the beach and the snow.

I put on my boots, not the best for snow walking, but I'll manage. Then I put on my jacket and pack myself warm. As I leave the apartment, I can see my breath and I laugh.

It really is freezing cold, but today, that just makes me smile. I wouldn't be me if I didn't do things the impractical way, like getting snowed in when on an island that I used to visit only during the summer.

It's a totally different experience being here right now, and that fits me fine. A different experience for a totally different time in my life. It's fitting.

Summers changed my life the first time around, making me realise and letting me explore my sexuality and my personality, but being here now, it makes me explore who I am as an adult, the new me, the person I grew up to be.

And that person has a new goal, a new plan. That person fell for Josie all over again, and doesn't want to let her go a second time.

12

❄

Josie

The clinic is quiet for a Monday morning, although, I think that may partially be because it's the day before Christmas, so most people are very busy with things related to that. This morning, I had just one appointment for a dog who had to get his check up and vaccinations for the year, and he was very helpful and sweet about it all, so it was all taken care of in no-time. The owner was very much in the holiday spirit, chatting about their plans for the next couple of days and asking me about mine. I smiled at them and made more of my own basically non-existent plans than they really were. Because I didn't want to dampen their mood.

Eline comes in with a plate full of Christmas cookies, smiling broadly as she puts them down on my desk. "To lift the spirits." She picks up a cookie herself and takes a bite of it. They're candy cane shaped with some in red and white and others in green and white. I do have to agree that it looks very festive.

I pick up a red one. "You made these yourself?"

She nods, grinning. "Yeah. This weekend. Made a *lot*, but the rest are for the actual holidays, not for snacks before then. But I thought that bringing some here would be a good idea." She takes another bite. "Oh, you can keep any that are left over. I really don't need to take them home." She's grinning and I can imagine how many tubs full of these she'll probably have at home.

"Thanks. But I'm really not that pathetic. I'll have fun, cuddle up with Bente, drink wine, watch a movie, things like that." Although, the plans I used to have do sound a lot more fun, but that can't be helped anymore, not really. Plans change, these obviously did.

"I know. Not saying that you are. Just offering a little Christmas spirit. You know?" She shrugs. "There is another appointment in half an hour for a rabbit and then the walk in hours start. Do you want to look over some cases for the rest of the week or something else before all that?" She pushes away from the table and steps behind me, reaching for my mouse and moving to the schedule for the week. "We have a dog coming in for a puppy scan tomorrow. So, that's fun. And then there are just some routine things. The days after that are mostly still free."

"Puppy scan, eh? Yeah, that sounds fun." At least a little light right now. Puppy scans are always fun and always make me smile. If the puppies are well, of course. But I recognise the name of the dog, and she's had two previous litters, all healthy and strong.

"Good. Now, what are we going to do right now?" Eline looks at me.

"I'm going to read up on some cases, because some of these are mostly from Loes, and since she's not here right now... I'll have to know about them. And you... I'm pretty sure you've got some things to do yourself." Right as I say it, the phone rings and Eline darts out of the office with a grin.

"Don't overwork yourself," she calls out over her shoulder as she closes the door behind her.

Yeah, yeah. I'm not going to overwork myself. As I open one of the case files, a very old cat with kidney problems, I also check my phone, but apart from the message from earlier this morning, I don't have any new messages from Sanne. I shouldn't be bummed out by it, I'm at work, I should be working and such, but I'm still a little bummed...

Then I send Kara a message. 'Hey, seems I have a huge change in plans for Christmas. What are you up to?'

I start reading the case file, my eyes scanning over the pages so that I'm sure that I remember the most important things, until I get a message back.

'Where are you? Did it not work out with the sexy girl?'

I wish that was the problem... 'Loes broke her arm this weekend. So I'm at home, well, at the clinic. Left the sexy girl on the island.'

This time the reply is faster. 'That is some severe bad luck! What are you going to do now?'

'I'm not sure yet. Probably just stay in and drink and read books or something.' I don't want to go travel all over the place, staying at home, especially wit this snow, is generally the best plan. And right now also suits my mood just fine.

'Well, Loes and the others are supposed to be coming over to my place tomorrow. But...' Of course, she stops the message there.

'But?' She's really mean.

'We could move it to your place? Your kitchen is bigger, you have better places for guests to crash, and for people to park...' Normally I don't celebrate Christmas on actual Christmas day with our friends, as I'm always at my family, having dinner there, but even though I'm back home now, I don't want to spend it with them. Getting away from them was the whole purpose of the trip to the island in the first place.

'I'm working all day tomorrow. I can't help you in any way.'

'That's okay. I can take care of that myself. It's not like I don't know your place almost as well as my own...' Kara stays over a lot here, since her small apartment in the city is far from what she likes. So, we spend a lot of time here together especially when we're planning on going on walks with Bente and Tys.

'Fine.' I nod, even though she can't see it.

'Are you sure?'

'Yeah. Tell everyone to come to my place. I'll check that we've got enough beds for people to crash later today.' I'm smiling a little now. Spending time with our friends may not have been the plan originally, but I guess it's still better than being all on my own.

'Cool. I'll let them know. We're going to get your mood back up. No more moping around and grumpy looks. I'm going to make you smile again.'

'How do you know I'm supposedly moping around?' She didn't even know that I was at home yet and not still on the island, right?

'Eline messaged me, about 10 minutes ago. If you hadn't messaged me, I would have messaged you.' Hey, at least she was open about ganging up on me with my assistant...

"Eline!" I can't help but call her out. "I'm not moping, stop saying that to Kara."

There are quick footsteps to the door and then Eline opens it, grinning widely. "Kara is such a snitch sometimes. And, you were moping and you're welcome." Then she closes the door again before I can even answer her.

Great...

Sure, it's good that I have friends who are trying to be helpful and caring, but sometimes... Sometimes I wonder how I even got 'adopted' by all of them. I guess it's okay, since I don't have any other plans for tomorrow anyway.

Maybe spending my time with my friends will make me feel less alone.

Maybe...

But I also acutely miss Sanne. Even though the fantasy was only there for a few days, I really wanted to celebrate Christmas with her. Watch her eyes light up and her smile broaden as I reveal all the food to her, and then maybe cuddle up on the couch for some fun times after everything…

But I guess some things just stay dreams…

In the evening, I'm back at my place, digging through the freezer to find something that I feel like eating, but nothing appeals to me. Maybe just a sandwich with cheese will have to do. It's not like I won't be eating my own weight in really delicious but bad for my health food tomorrow, or probably the days after, from all the leftovers.

I grab my phone, sending Sanne a quick picture of my dinner. 'Not feeling very festive.'

Her reply is pretty fast. 'No food in the house?'

'Not really feeling like anything.' I slide onto the couch and grab my ereader, pulling up a book.

'Poor you. I'm not much better. Just a little more fancy though, sandwich with fried egg.'

I grin. Of course, I'd left eggs behind. Well, it's still a little more fancy that what I have now. 'They keep you warm on the inside.' I don't even know where my brain is going with that right now.

'That, they do. But they're not as warm as you are.' My heart skips a beat at the words. I wish I could be with her right now. Right there with her. But we're not anywhere even close to being in the same place.

'Nothing is as warm as me. I'm hot.' I grin at my own words.

'Of course, you are. Although... I've not been able to test that theory lately. We'll have to test that when I see you next.'

My body starts to heat up just at the thought of touching her, holding her again, putting my hands to her bare skin. 'I'll hold you to that.'

'I'm counting on it. Maybe I should bring some ice cream over too, to cool you down after everything.'

What? 'Ice cream? In this weather?' I shiver just at the thought.

'Good point. We could just go outside and play in the snow instead.'

I have no idea where her mind is going right now. But it still makes me laugh, and of course, miss her even more. The weekend was like a dream and now the dream is over. But it's not like I can invite her over for Christmas, she's still on the island, and I'm at home, not there. I can't make her give up her holiday just because I would like to see her again.

'Oh! I took some pictures at the beach today. The sky was blue for a while, and it was so pretty.' She sends me some pictures and I have to agree, the blue sky with the white ice and the grey sea, it makes for an amazing sight. I miss being there when I look at the picture, it's just so special.

'Pretty! I hope you didn't freeze?'

'Not too badly. Just a little cold.' She sends some winking smileys with it. 'I'm warming up now.'

'Good.' I smile. Then Bente comes over and I ruffle my fingers through her fur. "With you around, I don't freeze, you know?" Bente looks happy, but, of course, that doesn't mean a thing, she's always happy when I give her attention.

'I'm going to get some more knitting in now. Talk to you later.'

I know that messaging is definitely not the same as just sitting next to each other and talking, and I really should distract myself for a while, at least until I go to bed and finally go to sleep. Today was exhausting, but it's still a little too early to go to bed. That, and Bente still needs to go out later. 'Talk to you later.' I put my phone away and curl up with the ereader, opening a new book, trying to get in the mood for more.

Tomorrow, Kara will come over to set up the kitchen and dining room here and then later, our friends will arrive too. I know I should be more excited about that than I really feel right now, but I just don't know. I had plans, and those kind of fell into nothing, and now I'll be spending it with friends, and even though I really like them, it's not the same as being able to spend the holidays with Sanne.

Close, but not the same, not by far.

My phone starts ringing, and I pick up, noticing it's Kara. "Hey."

"Hey. Are you excited for tomorrow yet?" She *does* sound very excited though.

"Sort of." I smile, happy to hear her so upbeat.

"I'll change your mind about that tomorrow. I promise!" I can hear the way Kara is grinning.

"What did you have in mind?" Sometimes she has the worst best-ideas.

"You'll see tomorrow. But I can promise you that it's good. Very, very good. Also, how much space do you have in your freezer? I may have to store a few things there during the day."

"It should be almost empty, not much there." I look around the room. "You can redecorate around here too, but you can't move everything around into some silly pattern or whatever." She did that once for a party...

"I know. I know. I promise. Just some decorations, nothing too bad."

"Define 'not too bad'." I narrow my eyes at nobody in particular.

"Glittery garlands? Some other decorations? Nothing that can break or shatter. I promise." She knows me too well.

"Fine." I shake my head.

"I promise that it will be fun. I know we weren't your first choice, but it'll be great. Really."

Yeah, yeah. I know all of that, it's just the not-being-with-Sanne that's being the downer on my mood.

"I'll have cookies?" I hear her grin, and she knows I can't resist.

"I'll forgive anything for your cookies. As long as you leave some at my office before you go into the house."

"Deal."

"Deal." I start to grin more.

Maybe tomorrow won't be that bad… Maybe. Maybe things will start to look up. Double maybe.

But maybe is still better than nothing, that's for sure.

13

❄

Sanne

Hiding where I was from Josie last night didn't feel right, it felt a little wrong even. But I know that if I'd told her where I was, or my plan, that she would have stopped me, that she would have insisted that I not go back home, that I was supposed to stay on the island, no matter her feelings towards me... Or my feelings towards her. She would have told me that being on holiday is more important than just a little Christmas or whatever.

Cleaning the apartment and getting rid of all the mess was easy enough. And then going home, which was a little sad to do, but the views of the snow and ice were amazing, which did distract me for a good while. That, and scrolling through recipes I could make for Christmas dinner on my phone...

I have no idea what to choose, what would even be a good idea to make. I know that I won't have much time today to buy and/or prepare any food, so nothing that would take hours and hours to simmer or that would require me hours and hours of hunting down ingredients. But I also can't make too little, that would make me feel just as crappy... I want this to be special, I want this to be very, very special.

But I'm not very good at that, romantic and special things, and I'll never be able to match those romance books she reads... No grand gestures from me, not really anyway.

I check my list with things I need to go buy.

Normally, when you do Christmas dinners with the whole family, everyone makes a few different recipes to combine for the whole meal. I tend to get caught with the starters or the dessert, since my parents don't do a huge Christmas so they tend to take the main course and I'm left with the start and finish, and my ex' family was pretty big and had a pretty set division of tasks, so we had little choice and tended to be the ones having to take care of random little things. It's not like I'm a good enough cook to make the main meal for thirty or so people anyway... I don't have imagination or patience enough for that. But it did always make me feel a little like we were just add ons, not part of the main event.

For tonight's dinner we're starting with a spicy tomato soup, with a paprika twist, then a main course of stuffed paprikas and baked salmon and some other veggies I can get my hands on, and a dessert of trifle. Of course, I'll need some wine and things like that for drinks and then probably a few other bits and pieces to finish it all off. But those meals will be the main things for tonight. I think I can manage it, hopefully.

Of course, after I finish shopping, I'll have to see if I should make this all at home, or if I should see if I can sneak into Josie's place and make everything there. I think that maybe the second option will be better, since it will also let me decorate her house, but then, I have no idea how to actually get into her place without tipping her off...

Although, she has her clinic at her house, and there should be someone taking care of the main desk there, right? I could try to get in that way and just hope that whoever mans the desk won't rat me out.

That would be a possibility, and I'm actually liking that idea better than the alternative, driving across the city with a pan full of hot tomato soup in the back of my car...

Definitely a better idea, and the second option is always good for backup.

I'm standing in line at the tills. All the tills are manned, and there are still eight people waiting for each one. Going shopping on Christmas day is not a good plan, and I'm obviously not the only one doing full shopping on the actual day itself. There are a lot of people with just one or two items in their baskets, probably something they'd forgotten to buy before, but there are also a lot of people with their carts full, like mine, who either had nothing at home, or way too little...

I check my phone, my eyes going down the list of ingredients, mentally crossing off each one against the items in my cart. So many things!

I let out a deep breath, I can do this. I can definitely do this. Probably.

As I was shopping, Josie had sent me a message saying that she was at work, and that she was a little bored. I sent her one of yesterday's pictures of the beach, hoping that she wouldn't catch that it wasn't from today... I don't want to lie, but I do want to surprise her. And if I let anything slip about not being on the island anymore, she will know immediately.

There are still three people ahead of me in the line, everyone getting grumpy and everything. Well, yeah, this is definitely not the right place to be today, but blaming other people for things going slow. The complaining people showed up here themselves, they can't blame others for doing the same thing. I don't get it, they gain nothing by complaining, just making other people more grumpy too, but somehow it's not their own fault that they're here.

Right…

When it's finally my turn, I try to get everything through as quick as I can. It's early in the afternoon and I still have a lot of food to prepare and things to decorate. I've got my car full of Christmas decorations, I got the boxes from storage last night, after I got home. That was after I had realised that I had no idea about Josie's decorations, so taking my own would probably be a good idea.

Somehow, I think that I may be over thinking it, but at the same time, how else am I supposed to do these things? How else am I supposed to prepare a Christmas dinner when I have no ideas about the place I'll be going?

Sure, finding out about the situation beforehand would have been a great idea, but that wasn't possible without tipping Josie off about my idea…

The trip from the store to the car is long and slow as I push the cart through the muddy snow, my feet sometimes losing a little grip. Luckily, I remembered to put boots on, with good grippy soles, instead of nice shoes. And if I'll be inside the house most of the time anyway, it doesn't matter so much what they look like, I can show off my warm and soft Christmas socks. Or, well, that's the explanation in my own head...

This is scary and exciting. Not knowing and still trying to plan things. I'm not normally that impulsive when it comes to these things. I can be super impulsive sometimes, but I also don't want to be intrusive, so doing something like this, surprising someone... Not really one of my strengths.

I bring the cart back to the rest and then get in the car, first turning on the heating, trying to warm up a little. I'm so, so cold! I like the idea of snow on Christmas day or evening, but I don't like the actual cold that comes with it. Makes my fingers so stiff and makes being outside so much more complicated and frustrating. Nope, not my favourite.

I check my phone one last time, checking the directions of how I'll get to Josie's place. It was pretty easy to find her clinic and then from there to finding out how to get there. And since she lives in the same place, easy directions. I just have to follow the road ahead of me, and then two traffic lights down, I have to turn left. But after that... After that things get a little more confusing, according to the map.

I put the phone in the holder in the car, hitting the button for it to give me the directions, and then I back out of my parking spot carefully, trying not to hit any people, or cars. It would be a good idea if everyone would be able to spend their Christmas all safe and healthy, not with bumps and bruises...

"Please turn left in twenty metres," the voice from my phone tells me.

Well, yeah, obviously, since that's the only way to get out of this car park…

"Your destination is on your right side. Please turn right in ten metres." The directions are starting to wear me down, especially since I can already see where I'm going, but since I don't want to let go of the wheel in this slippery weather, I've not turned the directions off yet. Getting here was easier than I thought it would be, the roads here weren't as complicated as they looked on the map. On the map it looked like a maze of roads, but in reality it was just some cycling paths that crossed the main road a few times and then a smaller road next to the main one...

I quickly check for pedestrians or bikes, before I turn onto the driveway of the clinic. Well, there is only a single driveway, so I presume it's for the clinic and the house at the same time. There are already a couple of cars in front of me, so I park as close to the side as possible, making sure not to be in anyone's way.

Then I get out, looking around. It's so open and quiet here, and very chilly, with the wind blowing across the fields too. *Brr.*

I can see the entrance to the clinic a little ahead of me, but next to me are footsteps going around the back of the building, not very many footsteps, and since it's not the clinic entrance, I suppose it's probably how to get to the house instead.

I could chance it... I don't know why, but instead of my original plan of going to the clinic to get the key or whatever, I follow the footsteps.

When I turn the corner around the building, on my right is a wide view over the fields, it's stunning and so open, and on my left I look into a homey living room, looking all cosy and everything.

I keep walking and inside the house I can hear two dogs bark. Ehm, I thought Josie only had Bente? Why are there two dogs?

Maybe this wasn't such a good idea after all?

I'm about to walk away again, I should probably check in at the clinic first, when I hear a door open behind me, and someone calls out. "Hello? Are you lost?"

When I turn around, a woman is standing a little behind me. She looks like she's right at home here, in a comfortable and warm sweater and wearing clogs. She's looking a little suspicious at me though. Did Josie already find someone else to spend Christmas with? *Uh, oh.* "Ehh... I'm... Ehhh." Then Bente rushes around her legs, and even though she tries to catch her, Bente is too fast, pushing against my legs all actively. I lean down and give her scratches. "Hey, girl. Are you so happy to see me?"

"Are you by any chance the woman Josie messaged me about over the weekend?" I can hear a little suspicion in her voice.

Josie messaged someone about me? It shouldn't give me butterflies in my stomach like it does, should it? "I'm Sanne. We used to..." I shrug, not exactly sure how to explain the way Josie and I are connected or how we know each other.

The woman grins smugly at me, like she's amused and not exactly surprised by me being here. "Of course. The one time Josie runs into an old lover, the lover follows her home."

Lover? What? How much does this woman know? "I'm sorry. I'd hoped to..." I sigh. "You're obviously already here. I'll leave."

"Oh, no. Don't go." The woman reaches out, grabbing the sleeve of my jacket. "I'm Kara, just a friend of Josie's. Don't go. She's been grumpy ever since she came back from the island, I think it's great that you're here."

I can't help smiling a little, it's stupid to feel happy about that, right?

"Me, Josie and some of our friends, are celebrating Christmas here because Josie has the biggest place of all of us. It was a last-minute change, I kind of forced it on her. I'm sure that she'd want you to be here too." Kara smiles softly. "And, honestly, I think I could use some help setting everything up. The others aren't coming here for another couple of hours, and I've got a lot of things to prepare."

"I've got food and decoration things with me too, but I don't have enough for more than just two people, I think." Spending Christmas here sounds great, but I really didn't bring enough to make meals for more than two people, and it would look strange to have small portions of a few things with everything else going on. Right?

"No worries. We're all doing something small, and I've got a list of everything everyone is making, so we can figure something out. I'm sure of it." Kara tugs on my arm a little. "Come on, it's cold out."

"I've still got things in the car." I point, but Kara is

pretty strong as she tugs me along.

"It's not going anywhere and it can't go bad, not with this cold." She smiles. "We're going to warm up first. And I want to know everything about the woman who can get Josie all up in knots."

I just walked straight into this, didn't I? I've just met the 'way too friendly' and 'way too nosey' friend. Although, this can be an advantage, when she's trying to ask me things, I can find out more about the 'adult Josie' from her.

"Sure. I could use something warm." This could be an even more interesting evening than I originally thought. Maybe not as intimate, but probably still a lot of fun.

14

Josie

I'm typing up some reports from hand written notes that I should have typed up a long time ago, but finally have the time for, or, at least, made the time for. Today is a very quiet day, apart from one or two appointments later on, I'm mostly here just to man the place in case we get an emergency call or something like that. That, and there are always things to do around here, things we often keep putting off when we can. Days like today are very good for backlog work.

Just before lunch, Kara came in and got the key to the house from me so that she could start preparing for dinner, and about ten minutes ago she sent me a message and insisted that I wasn't allowed to come check on her, that she wanted to keep everything a surprise or something like that. The idea was, no coming into the house until work is over, basically.

I don't know, I don't have a clue with her sometimes. Sometimes she gets these strange ideas and the best I can do is just to let her be, not to interfere too much. Her ideas are usually good ideas anyway, so it's not too bad... Usually.

I make sure to save the document of the case I was working on, and put my notes aside, making sure to put them away in the right folder so I won't lose them. Then I grab the next folder I need to work on. Why I always put this off, it often makes me question my own sanity, but then... I don't like doing this, so I don't really want to work on them, and that makes me not to want to work on them, and not actually doing it... Yeah, it keeps going round and round and just doesn't get done in the end.

There is a knock on the door.

"Yes?" I look up.

Eline opens the door and looks at me, smiling. "The owner with the dog with puppies is here a little early. Do you want to see her now or wait?"

I stand up, grabbing my coat. "Let's do it now. I can imagine she'd want to be back home again as soon as she can." The puppies are supposed to be born soon anyway, this is just to check that everything is going well. It should just be a quick scan before they're off again. I follow Eline to the waiting room, immediately spotting the heavily pregnant dog, and her broadly smiling owner. "Welcome, great to see you two. If you want to, you can follow me to the examination room."

The woman nods and the dog immediately gets up, standing close to me as I pet her softly.

"How is she doing?" We walk to the examination room.

"She's doing well, for her state, and in this weather." The owner nods. "She doesn't really want to go outside, but I get that. It's not been a real bother or issue, but I just think she's more comfortable in front of the radiator right now, staying warm."

"I can imagine." I pet the dog again and then I kneel down, running my hands over her. "You seem to be holding up pretty well, lady." I run my hands over her stomach carefully, trying to feel if everything is right. Then I stand up again. "Looks good. Let's get her on the table so we can take a closer look and make sure everyone is doing as well as they look."

I love puppies, and I love seeing them grow over time. It's beautiful, and they're so adorable.

I do hope to have a litter with Bente somewhere in the next year or so, I'd really like to experience that once with her, even if we don't do it again after that. It's just... I think it'll be fun and interesting.

But today, it's this lady in front of me who is having the

puppy experience.

The puppies looked very well and the dog was so enthusiastic and happy constantly. Apart from her big belly, it was hard to see that she was actually pregnant and in her final days or week of the pregnancy, she was just so energetic and excited. You don't see that very often, most dogs get very exhausted near the end.

I smile as I fill out the notes for the appointment, doing them in one go right now, instead of putting them aside first. If all dogs could be this happy and helpful while pregnant, that would at least make part of my job a lot easier.

It also makes me want to hug Bente, hold her. Normally, we'd go for her afternoon walk right about now. But I just spotted Kara with Bente and Tys, as I came back into my office, watched them walk off for the walk. So I don't even get to do *that* today...

Sigh.

I get up, going over to the front desk, catching Eline's eye. "Anything important for me to do?"

She grins at me evilly. "Always. But the question is if you want to do it?"

I groan, going over to her desk. "No more admin work, please."

She nods. "Fine. I have a case that Inge sent over for

you to maybe take a look at. It's about a very young cat who's not feeling too well and they can't seem to figure out what's wrong with her."

"I remember that." Inge asked me to take a look at the case, since she was stumped.

"She added the new lab results and they really have no clue at this point. She asked if you may be able to make more sense of them." Eline frowns. "I know, not the happiest case to work on today."

I frown too. "I know. But I'll take a look now. Kittens shouldn't be feeling poorly, maybe I can spot something new. Do I have any more appointments for today?"

Eline checks the monitor and shakes her head. "Nothing planned."

"Okay." I take the folders she's holding out for me. "Do you want to take a look at this together?" She may be my assistant, but she still has a lot of experience and knowledge, and two sets of eyes are better than one. That, and I don't really want to be alone right now, loneliness is bad.

"Yeah." She grabs the phone from the front desk and we go into one of the meeting rooms behind the front desk. That way we can still see people come in and she can answer the phone when needed.

I spread the different folders on the table. "Where did you want to look first?" We've talked about this case before, Inge brought it to my attention last week, before I left for my trip. It's a young kitten, just a few months old, and he keeps puking, but seems to have an appetite and also still uses the litter box like normal. They've mostly ruled out an infection and most common sources of these issues... But new ideas haven't been formed yet.

"Can I get the X-rays?" She sits down on one of the chairs and I hand her the pages.

Then I sit down too, with the most recent lab results in my hands, putting them next to the ones from three weeks ago, grabbing a few pens from the pile in the middle of the tables. Let's see if I can figure this out, or at least some of it...

I may not be able to spend my Christmas with the person I really wanted to spend it with, but at least I get to do what I like to do most. Help a small creature feel better again, and hopefully I'll be able to help out even a little, helping the owner of this little creature to get a better start of the next year, if this year isn't ending that well. It may not be an immediate solution, but we can work towards finding one anyway.

Helping furry critters isn't just my job, it's my passion.

I guess that's also a good way to spend my Christmas, even if it wasn't the one I planned, exactly.

Loud buzzing pulls me from my thoughts, making me drop my pen with which I was making notes. I blink, my head totally filled with thoughts that I don't know how to get back into the normal order.

"Eline! Josie!" Someone is calling from the front desk and ringing the buzzer again.

Eline jumps up at the other end of the table, a grin spreading over her face. "Loes!"

Loes? I blink, still a little dazed. I stand up too, not expecting Loes here today. Then I follow Eline, who is giving Loes an awkward hug.

"Happy holidays." Loes grins my way and behind her, her husband Jurre is holding a big bag with things.

"Happy holidays." I get closer, but with Loes' arm all up in a cast and everything, I don't think it's the best idea to give her a hug. "What are you doing here?"

"What am *I* doing here? Kara invited us over for dinner, she said we were celebrating it here. We are, right?" She's looking a little confused now.

"Yeah. Yeah, we are." I nod, taking a deep breath. "Sorry, I was..." I shake my head, trying to get rid of the last fuzziness.

"Working?" She grins.

"Yeah." I look around. "It's already that time then?" It was only one in the afternoon just moments ago...

Loes eyes Eline. "She's been all wrapped in work again?"

Eline grins. "Yeah."

"Josie..." Loes sighs. "You know that you work too hard, right?"

"I know." I close my eyes for a moment. "Anyway, Kara is already at the house, getting things ready. I'm just going to clean up here and I'll be joining you soon."

"Fine." Loes grins. "But if you take more than half an hour, I am going to come pick you up here personally." She levels a look at me.

I pointedly look at her arm. "I don't think you can."

"I can." Jurre winks at me. Well, yes, she's definitely big enough to pick me up...

"True." I take a deep breath. "I'm just going to round up the files and then close the place for the night. I won't be long. I promise." Then I look at Eline. "You can go with them if you want to."

She raises her eyebrow at me but then nods. "Sure. I'll turn off my computer and then I'll see you at home." She goes over to her computer and I go back into the meeting room, grabbing the files of the kitten case and sorting them so that I can easily find everything again tomorrow or whenever I look at them next.

I hear the door of the clinic close behind my friends and sit down on a chair, my heart heavy. It was nice to be so wrapped up in work that I hadn't realised time passed, but now that the Christmas dinner is starting, I know that I'll be surrounded by people I love, but without the one person I really want to spend it with.

Loes is here with her husband, Kara is on her own, but she doesn't seem to mind, Eline's girlfriend will show up soon too and then there are Arjen and Marco who have been together for probably as long as I know them, which has been ever since university... I'll be surrounded by happy people, and I'll have to act like I'm just as happy as they are, no matter what.

I hope Kara got us some good wine, I think I may want to be a little tipsy with all of that happiness around me. I'm not normally a grump on the holidays, but I may be today... *Sorry in advance, guys!*

I grab my phone and send a message off to Sanne. 'What are you doing tonight?'

Her reply is pretty fast. 'Eat food, drink? I don't know. You?'

I grab the folder with the kitten case from the table and bring it over to the front desk. Eline will put it away when she comes back in tomorrow, or I will, whatever. 'Spending the evening with friends. Also, lots of food.' I know that the food will be really good too, knowing my friends. 'What are you having?' I go over to my office, turning the computer off there and then checking I've turned all the machines and other things off too before I turn off the lights.

'Tomato soup and some salmon and trifle and a few other things.' Nice!

'That sounds really good.' And I think I'm starting to get hungry. But thinking about Sanne also being on her own at the holiday apartment, or going out for dinner at a restaurant... It makes me sad. Although, imagining her not being on her own doesn't make me much happier either…

'I was hoping you'd say that.' *What?*

I blink as I turn the lights in the examination room off and make my way to the front door. 'Why?' What is she talking about?

I slip into my heavy boots and then turn on the alarm of the clinic before I close the door behind me.

Then I turn around, and as I'm about to go over to the house, meeting up with my friends, I spot someone standing at the corner, looking over at me and my heart skips.

Sanne! Sanne is here!

What?

15

❄

Sanne

The look on Josie's face as she spots me is indescribable. The way her eyes grow, her mouth opens and she falters a step. She definitely didn't expect me here. With that last message, I thought she would guess what was up, but I guess that she had no idea.

I walk over to her, reaching out and she takes my hands. "Wow." Her voice is breathy.

I grin. "Good surprise?"

Josie nods, then pulls me closer, wrapping her warm arms around me. "I didn't think I'd see you today."

"I didn't want to spend tonight alone." I wrap my arms around her too, her scent surrounding me and calming me down, making me comfortable, making me feel homely. Making me feel at home.

"Well, you definitely won't now." I can hear the laugh in her voice and when she lets me go, she's grinning. "How long have you been here?"

"Most of the afternoon? Even after Kara told you not to come into the house, I was so scared that you would and that it would spoil the whole surprise thing." Every time I heard something outside, my heart would start to beat faster. I didn't want to hide from Josie, but I also didn't want her to find out too early.

"She was in on it. Of course, that's why she sent the message…" Josie shakes her head, still smiling. Then she takes my hands, tugging a little. "I guess we should probably go inside? Into the warmth?"

"Not before one more thing." I lean in, and although her eyes grow for a moment, she meets me halfway. Her lips are warm and pliable, and let me in as she grips my hands a little more, pulling me close to her.

I didn't know how much I was missing this, kissing her. I cling to her as I explore her more, tease her, play together. She feels so good! She tastes so good! I could do this forever.

Then I pull back and our breathing is hard. Wow. This was really... *Wow*.

"Now, it's time to go inside. I'm freezing." I grin, pulling her along.

I've spent all afternoon cooking and decorating with Kara. I couldn't get as much out of her about Josie as I would have liked, but that's okay. It was fun and I've found that Kara is a very friendly and silly person. But when the others came in, all looking at me in confusion, probably wondering if I was here with Kara, I knew that I had to get to Josie first. I knew that I had to see her, if only to make everything a little less awkward...

When Josie opens the door to step inside, everyone is standing around in the hallway, waiting for us.

Josie lets out a groan. "Are you guys serious? Shoo! Go eat or something." She makes shooing motions at the others, while still grinning.

Everyone leaves the hallway, but Kara leans in the doorway to the kitchen, looking at us, a smug smile on her face.

"What?" Josie tries to glare her way as she's smiling.

"Nothing." Kara shakes her head. "Just not surprised that this happened. You've finally found someone who will put up with your workaholic antics." Then she turns around and closes the door to the kitchen behind her, leaving us alone.

When Josie looks up at me after taking her boots off, she's not smiling anymore. "I guess Kara is right about that." She sighs, her eyes sad. "I'm sorry. This… This is…" She shakes her head.

I step closer to her, reaching out to her again. "Don't apologise. I would be lying if I said that I didn't wish I could have kept you on the island, but you wouldn't be you if you hadn't gone home, and I wouldn't have been as…" I lick my lips, swallowing the words that almost slipped out. "I wouldn't have been a good friend if I would have let you stay when I know how important this all is to you. This is your work, your passion. I knew that. I know that."

She nods, sighing deep. "This will never end, you know that, right? Having to suddenly get up and get to the clinic because of an emergency, or being on call, those things?"

"I know. This is your work, your passion. But I'm here, aren't I?" I put my fingers to her lips. "I'm here. And right now, there is no place in the world I'd rather be."

The smile she's showing me is almost blinding, then she takes me in a tight hug and I lean against her, enjoying our closeness again. "Thank you." Her whisper is almost too quiet to hear, but I nod against her shoulder.

I really don't want to be anywhere else. Not only with Josie, but her friends also give this loving and welcoming vibe, this is exactly where I want to be, with the woman I still don't dare to confess my love to...

One step at a time.

Kara grins my way as we put the spicy tomato soup I had planned into small glasses, one for everyone. Then I put the glasses onto their own little plates and put some baguette slices next to them. We realised that we could make the soup much stronger than the recipe, spice it up more, and then just serve it as a small taster before the real starter. It came out pretty nicely, especially when Loes brought over extra baguettes and saved our day.

"We're a good team." Kara grabs four of the plates, holding them comfortably.

"Thanks. We are." I grab three more and then we make our way to the living room, where a huge table, well, actually, three tables with just a single tablecloth but whatever, is all set up with Christmas decorations, people already waiting for us.

I start putting some of the plates down and Kara does the same on the other side of the table.

"Now, while I'm grabbing the final items, Sanne can explain what it all is." Kara flashes me a grin as she quickly rushes off.

I roll my eyes, but then take a deep breath. I can feel Josie's eyes on me, her gaze intense and hot. "You have a spicy tomato soup, quite spicy, with some baguette and garlic butter. Enjoy."

Kara returns with the final plates with soup and the garlic butter, before we both sit down.

As soon as I sit down, Josie's hand is on my leg, squeezing a little as she leans close. "This looks really good. And I guess this is the soup you were talking about?"

"It is." I grin, enjoying her closeness, enjoying the way she smiles at me.

"How long have you been planning this? Because this looks planned." Josie looks over the table. When I eye her, I see no jealousy or whatever, just curiosity and surprise.

"No plans. I..." I lean closer to her, not wanting the others to hear. "I came back to the city yesterday. I'd planned out a whole meal for just the two of us, but then I found Kara already cooking when I arrived here this afternoon." I still feel my cheeks heat up just thinking about it.

Josie lets out a laugh. "Well, I'm happy either way. I wouldn't have minded spending Christmas with just you either." My heart flutters at the words. "Thank you. Thank you for being here."

"I wanted to be here. With you." I give her a quick kiss on her cheek and then dip some baguette in the soup, needing to give myself a little distraction, giving myself something to do so I won't keep kissing her.

When I glance her way, Josie grins too as she dips her bread into the soup and takes a bite, her eyes going wide for a moment and then she grins even more. "Oh, this is good."

"Sanne's recipe." Kara, who is sitting opposite us, grins.

"Really?" Josie raises an eyebrow as she glances my way.

My cheeks heat up. "Sort of. I found the recipe online and got the ingredients. It's not *mine* exactly."

"Still good." Josie winks. "This is a great start to the meal. Seriously."

"I agree," Loes also answers from Josie's other side. "If this is what you come up with. I want you here every time we're all bringing something to eat. This is so good."

"Hey!" Kara glares at Loes. "What about me? You said the same thing about my food."

"And I stand by that comment. Can't we have you both here?" Loes laughs and I can't help my own laughter.

This feels good. This happiness, this comfortable atmosphere, all of it. This feels so good. It's the first time in years that I don't feel awkward or uncomfortable being at a large table with people. Everyone here is just so nice and easygoing, it's easy to be around them.

It makes me happy.

Josie tugs on my arm. "Let's get the dogs something to eat and then take them for a walk."

We're waiting for the main course to be finished, Arjen and Marco are in the kitchen doing stuff. But apparently, that's going to take a while still. I guess going for a walk could be a good idea now, and Bente and Tys have been trying to beg food from everyone in the last twenty minutes. It didn't work, but that didn't stop them from trying, or trying to outdo each other...

"Sure." I get up and follow Josie, who is going into the kitchen, both the dogs following us. "They know what you're going to do." I grin as I watch her.

Josie looks my way, grinning. "They do know. I always get them food around this time. They learn fast, especially when it's about food."

Kara steps next to me, looking over the kitchen, watching Arjen stir something in a huge pan. It smells great. "Josie always escapes for a while. She likes the quiet."

"Hey!" Josie pretend-glares her way. "Feeding the dogs makes me sound sweet and a little cool. What you're saying doesn't." She takes both bowls and Bente and Tys immediately sit down, their eyes locked on the food.

Then Josie puts them down, one side of the kitchen for Bente and the other side of the kitchen for Tys.

Kara bumps her shoulder into mine. "I don't think trying to look cool is going to be a problem. Not with the way this one looks at you."

My cheeks heat up fast and so do Josie's cheeks as she looks my way.

"Let's... Ehh... Let's put our coats on." I go into the hallway, trying really hard not to blush even harder.

I still hear Kara's laugh behind me, then a soft sound and the laughing stops, before it starts again. I don't know what happened, but I'm pretty sure that I don't need to know.

As I'm putting my jacket on, I spot my bag with Josie's gift in the hallway. Should I...

Josie comes into the hallway too, the dogs following her.

"That's fast." I grin.

"That they are." She grabs her boots and then her jacket.

"Ehmm." I let out a deep breath. "Do you guys do presents or anything?"

Josie looks up at me, smiling softly. "Nah. Why? You don't have to be scared that you don't have anything for them."

"Actually..." I reach into my bag, pulling out the

present. "I have something for you." I hold it out awkwardly.

"Oh." Her eyes grow as she accepts it. "I don't have anything for you, though."

I shrug. "That's okay. This was just a silly idea of mine."

"Can I open it?"

I nod. "I think it'll be a good moment to open it, right about now."

Josie raises her eyebrow at me, but doesn't ask anything else. When she takes the paper off, her eyes start to shine, until she holds the hat in her hands. Then she meets my eyes, hers filled with an emotion I don't know how to read, but it seems like a good emotion. "You made this yourself?"

I nod, my cheeks all hot.

"When?" She turns it around in her hands a few times.

"Over the weekend. Finished it yesterday on my way home." I look at my hands, not sure I dare to meet her eyes.

"It's beautiful." Then I'm in her arms again, and she's squeezing me tightly. "Thank you so much! I'll wear it immediately!"

I grin as I watch her put it on. The dark red of the hat matches the sweater she's wearing right now, I couldn't have planned it any better if I had...

"Thank you." She gives me a quick kiss, but then Bente pushes between us. Her eyes go down to Bente. "I think we may need to actually go walk them now, though."

"Maybe." I grin. This was a good idea, a really good idea.

Josie leans closer. "Are you staying the night?" Her voice is low, giving me butterflies in my stomach.

"I think I may be?" What's going on in her head?

"I guess I know what present to give you later, then." The heat in her gaze suddenly makes me wish that this whole party was already over, but I know that it'll take a whole lot longer.

Wow. I guess Josie really still has ways to surprise me, or make my body react exactly in the ways that she wants.

And I want her to, too.

16

Josie

Kara wasn't wrong when she said that I prefer to take a break from everyone about halfway through the meal. I'm just really not that good with groups of people for a longer time span.

But taking Sanne out into the fields, getting some time with her to myself, well, that's definitely an advantage today.

And the hat she made me, so soft and comfortable... I can barely believe it. I can barely believe that she'd make me something like this, out of nowhere. Sure, I know that we joked about her making me a sweater, but to get something so sweet... Not what I expected, at all.

I take her hand as we step on the road in front of the house, walking over it a short while to get to the path through the fields, where the dogs can go run all they like. Then I put both our hands into my pocket, hopefully keeping us both a little warm.

I can see our breaths as we walk in silence, just listening to the wind and the trees.

"It's very different here." Sanne's voice is quiet and almost filled with awe.

"From where?" I glance at her before looking ahead again.

"The island." She smiles. "No sea, and the wind isn't as rough."

"You should see it sometimes. It can get really rough here too." A shiver goes down my spine. The wind can get pretty bad here, depending on the direction it comes from.

"Maybe. But I like it here. Just enough wind and trees and snow."

"I agree with you on that." We turn onto a small path and I lean down, letting Bente and Tys go. "Go, run. Get all that energy out now."

They both race off. Shadows in the darkness as they race along the path. We follow them quietly, not saying anything, but I enjoy being here with Sanne, just being together. Would it be silly to think that I'd love to do this every evening? Every morning? Every day?

Probably...

"Your friends..." I watch the puffs of clouds coming

from Sanne's lips. "They're a lively bunch." She smiles at me and I smile back.

"They are. They're really friendly and they really love pulling new people along in whatever they're doing."

"I got that idea too." She starts grinning. "And Kara totally just does whatever she feels like doing. She seems very carefree."

"Yeah... She can definitely be. But she also always means well and tries so hard." Which is probably one of the reasons she wanted to celebrate Christmas at my place, keep me entertained and not just doing stuff on my own, being all grumpy as she would put it, not moping around.

"I know. I saw her." She lets out a short laugh.

"What?"

"Nothing." Sanne grins, then takes my hand and pulls me closer. "Just that you're amazing, and your friends reflect that."

"Nothing in comparison to you." I pull her the last distance to me, our lips touching. I'm kissing her again. I love kissing her so much, and I can't seem to get enough of it. There isn't much I want to do more in the world more than that, kissing Sanne, although... Maybe... Maybe there is.

I hear a lot of feet coming our way and Bente and Tys run around us, chasing each other, all happy.

I laugh and we start walking again. My feet are slowly

starting to freeze and we should probably not stay away for too long, with everyone still at the table and everything.

The main course is actually made up of a lot of smaller dishes, provided by everyone at the table. I remember Sanne saying something about salmon, but there is also some stew, a huge smoked ham and so many different little veggie dishes. I don't think we'll be able to finish this all today, or even this week…

I have no idea what to get first, but I don't really have to worry, as apparently I don't have to choose when people are all telling me that their dish is the best and I end up with a small piece of everything on my plate.

Being here, surrounded by everyone, this is what real family feels like, what real closeness and love feels like. And having Sanne next to me makes it even better, makes me feel even more complete.

It's strange how not having seen each other in over a decade still makes me feel these same things I used to feel when I saw her every summer. And I have no idea how these feelings will stay, but I also know that if I still feel like this now, after so much time, that this is probably something we should explore more. Right? We should probably not hide away from it all again... Probably.

I feel Sanne's gaze on me and when I look at her, she

smiles softly. "Hmm?"

"You seemed lost in thought."

I shrug. "Maybe a little. I think it may be the wine, making me all grown-up and contemplative." I take another sip, and I have to admit that Kara chose a great red wine to go with the dinner.

Sanne's eyes start to twinkle as she laughs. "Well, I don't know what will happen if you only drink that and don't eat anything, though." She winks.

"I'm fairly sure that I'm not drinking on an empty stomach right now." I wink back at her. "Between the soup and all the other little things from before, I'm already starting to get a little full..."

Sanne pretends to be offended, her eyes widening. "I do hope not. We've still got desserts left."

I let out a groan, and kind of mean it. I don't know if I can deal with desserts right now.

"Don't worry." Kara grins from the other side of the table. "We've got all evening, and night, if needed."

I close my eyes. We've got all evening, and I'm already starting to get full... How am I going to manage anything more?

I feel Sanne lean close. "I'm sure we'll figure something out. I can think of a few 'workout' things to get you hungry again…" Her voice is low, sexy, and I feel heat rush through my body in anticipation. Even if it's a silly thought, that does sound very very nice. 'Working out' is definitely one way to get an appetite, but with all the people here... I don't think we would be able to slip away for anything right now... Especially since everyone seems to be keeping their eyes on us...

I take a bit more of some roasted bell peppers and salmon. It tastes really good, and Kara is right, we've got all evening. We don't need to rush or worry. Everything will be fine, we're not going anywhere anyway. Not that we've planned…

Kara's eyes stay on me and I raise my eyebrow at her. "What's up?"

She shakes her head, smiling. "Nothing much."

"So there is *something*..." I can be annoying too, if I want to be.

She shrugs. "I saw an ad for a primary school teacher position on Schiermonnikoog starting in a few months." She keeps her voice low and I have no idea why, because this is so cool!

"Tell me more..." I lean in a little. "Did you apply for it yet?"

She shakes her head. "Not yet. I just... I didn't know if I should bother, if it's even a good idea."

Next to me, Sanne moves forward too. "Why not?"

"For how long is it?" Kara is a primary school teacher, but she's just a substitute teacher, so she doesn't have that stable of an income or really knows where she'll be needed next for the next weeks. I know she's tired of that life, and I also know that working on the island would be something she'd really love. Especially since it means she'd be able to walk Tys there all the time.

Kara sighs deep. "It's three days a week, from the end of January or start of February to about summer break. Something like that. One of their teachers is out with a burnout and another one will be going on maternity leave soon. So they need someone to cover a couple of days in the week." She shakes her head again, looking a little frustrated. "I don't know yet."

"Why not?" I grin. "You can always try and apply. You love the island, you're a great teacher, and I don't see a reason not to do it."

"I'll be away from everyone here." She looks around the table. "And it's not even that many hours, and I'd have to do something about living arrangements, and stuff like that... I don't know." She frowns, her mouth a thin line. She's scared, and I don't know what of.

"I could always come visit you." I wink. "Bente would love to be on the island more and it's a great excuse to not be in the clinic every weekend, as some people have been telling me not to do." I level a look at her.

She grins back at me. "That's all about you, not me. That makes it sound like you should go live there."

"I wouldn't mind," Sanne pipes up next to me.

I glance her way, not entirely sure that I heard that right.

"Really?"

She shrugs a little, smiling. "I don't know. It sounds fun. Although, I don't know if I'd be able to live there full-time."

I'd not considered that… "I can't leave my clinic here."

Sanne looks at me, winking. "I know. But we could still visit Kara often, right?"

We, she said it. She said that *we* could visit Kara. My heart does that skipping thing a few times as I glance her way. "We definitely could."

"Then, it's decided." Sanne grins, looking at Kara. "Now you will have to apply for the job. It's a great location to work. You love the island. You get to do all sorts of cool things. And it means that Josie has to get away from the clinic more often."

Kara grins at her, like I'm not even here, like they're not talking about me. "I guess those are good arguments. And you'd probably have a decently cheap place to sleep too, when you do visit."

"Problem solved." Sanne grins, then stands up. "I'll be right back." She goes towards the kitchen and probably the bathroom, between the wine and water and other things… Yeah.

"I like her even more now." Kara grins at me. "She's got great ideas."

"And she seems great at making people do silly stuff." I shake my head. Sanne fits in with everyone else so easily, like she's always been here with us, and it feels strange and so good at the same time.

162

"Maybe." Kara shrugs. "But I guess she's right. I can always try, I won't know if I don't try. I am tired of all this part-time and a different school every other week stuff." She takes a sip of her wine.

"I can imagine." I nod. "It's never really that easy, especially not knowing what and when."

"Yeah." She sighs. "And I'm tired of playing the whole 'keeping the company happy' thing, and always being on my toes when I'm at a new school..." She looks over the table. "I would miss everyone though."

I let out a laugh. "You're not gone yet. You've not even applied. Worry about the rest when all that's done. Not yet." I touch her arm. "It would be a great opportunity for you. You know that as well as I do."

Kara puts her hand over mine. "You're right. It would be." Her eyes are soft. "Don't let your own opportunity slip through your fingers either."

I nod. "I'm not going to."

She grins, an almost evil grin. "I knew it the moment you messaged me. You're just too dense sometimes..." Then she gets up. "I see that I should get some more wine, and water. I'll be right back."

I lean back in my chair as Sanne comes back into the room, her eyes on me, filled with joy and a spark of naughtiness, and my heart flutters, my stomach doing a flip. She sits down next to me, her hand on my thigh.

"You look happy." She's smiling as she leans close.

"I *am* happy." I take her hand and kiss her fingers.

"Thank you for surprising me today. Thank you for everything."

She shrugs a little, her face flushing. "I just..." She shrugs. "Just..."

I tug on her arm, making her come closer, and then I put my lips to hers, kissing her. She looks so cute when she's all flustered and doesn't know what to say. Just having her near me makes me happier than I've ever thought possible.

I'm not letting her get away again, I'm not going to let that happen again.

17

Sanne

It's about ten in the evening when the desserts finally arrive at the table. There are a lot to choose from, including the trifle I made. There are also Pavlovas and Christmas cookies and all sorts of chocolates and other things. I have no idea how we're going to be eating all of this. But I guess we're going to try very soon.

I put some of the trifle on my plate, eating all the different layers of it first, trying them all on their own before I mix everything together. I don't know how I managed to actually make it taste right, although, I'm pretty sure that Kara helping me out had something to do with it. I may not be the best cook, but Kara is definitely a much better cook than I am, no matter how much she keeps saying that she's not.

I had no idea that Kara also liked to go Schiermonnikoog. Although, since it's the island closest to our county, it makes sense. It makes a lot of sense that she'd take her dog there too, especially with the way that Josie keeps talking about the island and how great it is for dogs to run around.

But back there, it did look like Kara was just trying to come up with excuses as to why it wouldn't work, instead of why it would be a great idea that she could be working there. I may have been a little too enthusiastic, but that's how I am.

Josie taps on my arm, holding out a spoon with a mixture of what looks like half the desserts on it. "Try this."

"Why?" I eye her.

"Just try it." She's grinning. "I promise that it isn't bad. Really."

"Fine." I open my mouth, and she feeds me the bite. As soon as I close my lips around it, I can almost feel the different flavours in my mouth, not just taste them but almost feel them. I have no idea how or why, but it's an interesting experience. The trifle and Pavlova mix well, but I'm fairly sure she's mixed something else in with it too. Something alcoholic or something. After I've swallowed it down, I eye her. "What's in it?"

She flashes me a huge grin, teeth and all, it makes her

almost look like a kid. "Just some advocaat, not a lot, just a little. But it works, right?"

"Only in small quantities." I shake my head, also smiling. "It's too sweet otherwise, and the alcohol doesn't help it."

She shrugs a little. "Maybe. But it's not bad, right?"

"It's not too bad. I agree." Then I take a couple of sips of water, just to get the flavour out of my mouth, too overwhelming if I'm going to be eating the trifle again.

Josie keeps eating her concoction of whatever it is as I just look at her. When I meet Kara's eyes, she just shrugs, rolling her eyes a little.

"Don't ask me. That's not my influence." Kara takes a bite of a cookie before taking a bite of the trifle too. No... Definitely not... Why would anyone even think that?

I smile as I look at them. You can see that they've been friends for a long time, and they've obviously started to take over each other's habits. When we were young, Josie wasn't that good around a lot of people, sometimes I felt like I was the only one who was really her friend. But it seems that these days, she's got a lot more friends, all of them amazing and interesting people in their own ways.

For being with people I don't know very well, I feel at home here. Something that I don't even often feel when I'm actually at home, or with my own family. This is what it could also be like... This is what it could be like...

This is what I want.

After dessert, we've taken care of most of the dishes and have moved to the living room, sitting on the various couches and chairs, a low table in the middle of the place holding a variety of cookies and other snacks. Even more food. I'm full to bursting about now.

Josie wraps her arm around my shoulder, pulling me against her a little as we're curled up on the couch, under a blanket of course. The others are talking about work and other things, but I'm just sort-of listening to them, happy where I am, and slowly starting to doze off.

My stomach is full, I've had enough alcohol to feel a little buzz, and it's nice and warm here. That, and I'm here with Josie. All things that make me feel all warm and fuzzy, perfect to fall asleep.

Bente comes over to us, putting her head on the blanket over us, looking up, before carefully trying to crawl up on the couch with us.

"Uh-uh." Josie looks at Bente, and she puts her paw back on the ground as she keeps her head on the blanket, looking at me now, like I will allow her onto it instead of mean Josie.

I shake my head, smiling at her. "Nope. I'm not the one who you're going to have to convince."

She sits down, but keeps her head where it is, on the blanket, looking at us. Then Tys comes up to her and mirrors what she's doing, his head also on the blanket and I let out a laugh. It looks so silly. Two dogs trying their best at making us let them onto the couch.

"No." Josie shakes her head. "You've got your own pillow bed. I'm cuddling with Sanne over here." She pulls at the blanket and Bente just lets herself flop down onto the ground with a deep sigh.

I lean close to Josie. "I think she thinks you're mean."

Josie grins. "I'm pretty sure that she thinks I'm mean." Her fingers play over my arm, trailing up and down. "But I'm not giving up my spot with you, I can cuddle with her often enough."

I let out a short laugh, imagining Josie on the couch with Bente, like she's now sitting with me. "You do?"

"Of course." She tightens her arm around me. "She's warm, and cuddly, and a little needy." Josie leans closer. "And I will keep talking in this slow and low voice until you fall asleep if you don't watch out."

I glance up at her and her eyes are shining, filled with warmth and happiness. "You wouldn't."

"Oh, I would." She kisses the top of my head. "We may want to move to a different location before you fall asleep."

I glance around the room. "What about the others?"

"Oh, they know their way around the house. And they know where to find the bedrooms and the other things they need. Don't worry about them." Josie slowly gets up and I also get up from the couch. "We're off to bed." Josie takes my hand. "I'm sure this one needs to sleep now."

"Hey." I try to sound offended, but the yawn I let out doesn't make my case any better. "Night." I wave my hand to the room as Josie starts pulling me away.

"Night," the others call back.

"Have fun!" Kara grins, wiggling her eyebrows at me and I try to glare at her, but I'm just too tired for all of this now.

As Josie pulls me into the hallway and up the stairs, I remember the dogs. "Don't you have to walk with Bente still?" I look around, trying to figure it all out.

"Kara and the others will do that. Don't worry." Then we reach a fairly large hallway upstairs and I remember that this house is actually quite big in comparison to where I live. Josie taps on a door which has the image of a bath on it. "This is the upstairs bathroom. With bath, shower and toilet, if you need it."

"Right." I look at the door, but then she pulls me along again.

"And this is my room." She opens the door at the end of the hallway, right next to the bathroom.

When we step inside, it's all in soft and warm colours and has a lot of exposed wooden beams. Very pretty, at least, what I can grasp right now. It looks warm, and it feels warm too.

Then Josie closes the door behind me and wraps her arms around me, looking at me with a smile. "I've caught you." Her voice is low and sexy, making my insides squirm.

Suddenly, I'm not so tired anymore. Now I'm in Josie's bedroom, faced with a very sexy woman, who looks like she could devour me at any time, I'm not so tired anymore, and neither is my body, coming alive just under her gaze. Her eyes go over my face, like she's searching for something, and I wrap my arms around her too, slowly leaning closer. "I'm pretty sure you promised me a Christmas gift..."

"I did, didn't I?" She slowly puts her lips to mine, the kisses quick and soft, way too chaste for the fire building inside me.

"You did." I pull her against me more, trying to deepen the kisses, but she keeps pulling back just a little bit each time, teasing me. "And you're mean."

"Oh, I'm fairly sure that you'll call me much worse than that later." She flashes me a grin, but then her hand slides up, cradling the back of my neck and she pushes her lips against mine more, overwhelming me and making me gasp out. Then she's there. Tongue, teeth, lips, all teasing me, driving me crazy, driving my body crazy. She feels so good, she tastes so good, she smells so good. So, so good.

I grip her shirt, surprised by her sudden forwardness, enjoying it. I hold on, letting it come over me, losing myself in everything. Then her hand slides down, to my ass, and then up under my shirt. Her hand is on my bare back and I gasp out again. I want this so much, so, so much. I want more. I want her to touch me more, to hold me more, I want to feel her more.

Then she steps back, our breathing hard, and she looks at me, grinning. "You look beautiful."

I feel my cheeks trying to heat up even more than they already do, but I'm not sure that's even possible, and I may have lost my ability to speak already.

Josie reaches for my sweater, slowly pulling it over my head as I help her, and then I'm standing in a t-shirt and jeans, Josie looking at me, her eyes hot. The next moment she steps closer again. "I've been wanting to do this for days." Her voice is low and rough, and she plays her fingers over my bare arms, touching, caressing, sending shivers through my whole body, setting me on fire.

I slowly reach out to her too, trailing my fingers over her cheek. "Me too." I barely recognise my own voice, so low and filled with lust.

Josie nuzzles against my chin and then trails kisses

down my jaw to my neck. My thoughts wipe, getting so wrapped up in all the sensations that I can barely think anymore. She feels so good.

Her fingers slide away, and then they're under my t-shirt again, her hands on my skin, smoothing over it, slowly sliding up, her thumbs grazing the underside of my bra.

I let out a little gasp, my whole body wound tight.

"You're so amazing." Her voice tickles my neck, her breath hot on my skin. Then she reaches up higher and takes my boobs in her hands, fitting perfectly in her palms, and involuntarily I push closer, wanting her to touch me more. Needing her to touch me more.

"Josie..." It's almost begging, how needy my voice sounds.

She takes my t-shirt and pulls it off too, her eyes raking over me in my jeans and bra. The black jeans almost clashing with the bright pink and lacy bra, but the way her eyes darken tells me that Josie doesn't care. Where I see imperfections and silly clothing choices, her eyes linger, and she's smiling so sexily.

Then she reaches out again, admiring, but almost stronger than that, worshipping, and trails her fingers from the top of my jeans, over my definitely-not-slim stomach, up to my ribcage, ending at my bra, tracing the pattens of the lace for a moment. "You were beautiful before, but you've grown even more beautiful." She steps closer, planting a kiss right on one of my boobs, wrapping her arms around my waist, pulling me close, making me feel like the most beautiful woman in the world.

Like there is nothing better in the world than this.

18

❄

Josie

Maybe I'm sappy, but I think I've got the most beautiful woman in the world in my arms. I love how her ass fills out those jeans, her wide hips but her slim waist and then her boobs... Ten years ago, she was beautiful, but now, she's otherworldly in her beauty, a goddess like those luscious ones from ancient mythology, a woman made to be cherished and loved, to be worshipped.

I can feel her heart beat fast under my touch, her breathing shallow and the way her whole body is thrumming with energy.

I kiss down the mound of her breast to the top of her bra, slowly pulling the cup aside, and then I take her pebbled nipple in my mouth, sucking on it. She lets out a moan as her fingers tighten in my shirt, holding on. As I keep carefully sucking on her nipple, I make quick work of her bra, pulling it aside and taking her other breast in my hand, cupping the heavy flesh, a perfect fit.

She's so beautiful. I glance up at her face and she's biting her lip, her eyes closed as she's lost in the sensations.

I take her other nipple in my mouth, sucking on it before I take it between my teeth and roll it carefully.

"Josie." Her voice pitches, and her whole body jerks towards me, but she doesn't push me away, her fingers on my shirt only tightening, trying to pull me even closer. I play with one nipple between my fingers, I remember she used to be so sensitive and it seems like she's no different now, and go between sucking on and rolling the other nipple between my lips, as I slide my other hand down to her jeans, rubbing my thumb over her mound. She grinds against me, and I can almost feel the electricity building inside her.

Then I let her breasts go and kneel down, trailing kisses down her stomach until I reach her jeans, and there I stop, looking up at her.

I'm almost pulled out of it all, worried by the look in her eyes, the almost-tears there, then she flashes me a smile.

"I love you." Her voice is tick and rough, her fingers grabbing at me are jittery and I stand up, taking her in my arms as my heart bursts with feelings.

"I love you too. Always have." My voice is foreign to me, my own tears so close to the surface. I tighten my arms around her, holding her tightly against me. That was a surprise, way too much of a surprise…

"I love you." She repeats the words into my shirt as she pushes closer. "I couldn't let this all go by again. I couldn't let you go again." She slides her hands under my shirt, holding on to my bare skin and pulling me even closer if that's even possible. Then her lips are on mine, ravaging me, hungry, hungry like this night will never end, a deep insatiable hunger.

I keep holding her, giving as best as I can, because if I don't, she's going to swallow me whole, I'm sure of that.

I move us closer to the bed, trying to get us onto it so that we don't have to worry about being able to stand up and everything anymore. Then I slowly let her down on the bed, her eyes still on me.

I pull off my sweater and my shirt and jeans and climb onto the bed with her, helping her take her jeans off.

This is different now, everything feels different now. It's no more just about me showing her love, there is an urgency to our movements, like we have to keep moving, like we have to get naked as fast as possible, having to get to each other's skin as fast as possible.

Her hands roam over me, I'm not as feminine and curvy as she is, much more blocky, more muscles too, but the way her fingers trail over me, I don't think that there is any difference to it for Sanne. I push closer to her, to her in her lacy thong which matches the beautiful bright pink bra I got rid off before. I'm not wearing anything matching, I didn't expect anything. Although, it's all black, so I guess it could seen as matching. I don't know.

Then Sanne slides her thumb under the bottom of my bra, rubbing it against my breast, and I reach out to her, taking one of her breasts in my hand, leaning in to suck on her nipple again, but she pushes me onto my back, straddling me.

"My turn." She pulls down the cups of my bra, exposing my breasts, and then takes one nipple in her mouth as she rubs the other one, kneading it softly, touching me, sending sensations through my body.

I close my eyes, a soft gasp escaping my lips, and I wrap my arms around her waist, holding her close. Then she rocks her hips into mine, rocking us together. She feels so good, overwhelming my thoughts, overwhelming everything in me.

She slowly shimmies down a bit and reaches between us, sliding her finger over my thong, over the fabric, but still touching me, rhythmically rubbing, sending my brain in overdrive.

I pull her down next to me, one arm around her while

I trail my other one down her body, caressing every part that I can reach. Until I get to her thong, until I reach the last piece of clothing still on her, until I dip my finger under the frail fabric and touch her directly.

With a gasp, she rocks her hips into my hand, making me move harder, faster.

I grin, leaning closer to her and carefully kissing her, trying to keep the movements light, but that's no use when she slips her fingers under my thong too and touches me harder, putting more pressure, rubbing at exactly the right speed to make me lose my mind.

"Sanne." My voice is little more than a moan and I try to keep kissing her, our bodies pushed together, rocking together. Giving each other pleasure as we try to stay sane ourselves.

I trail my hand down her arm, to her amazing breasts and tweak her nipple just a little bit. Her hips move in response, a jerking movement, as she lets out a gasp and a low moan.

I do it again, never faltering my hand between her legs, trying to keep her on edge, teasing her nipple. And she moans out again, her body moving against my hands, her kisses going sloppy, until her breathing hitches and I can feel the way her whole body tightens and she lets out a deep gasp. I watch the pleasure go over her face, the way she goes up into the sensation, the view beautiful and so sexy.

Then she moves her hand faster against me, coming up a little on her arm and kissing my neck. Everything together, the way she's looking at me, the way she smells, the way she's touching me, it's all too much and I fall over the edge as I come, everything going tight and pleasure rushing through me. I'm blinded by the sensations for a moment, my breathing hard and I've got a tough time remembering anything but Sanne, and having her with me.

When I trust my body more, I pull her closer, taking her luscious body in my arms, and pull the covers over us.

She stirs a little, her head on my arm, her lips a fraction from my breast. "That was definitely the best Christmas gift I've ever had." She's smiling and I reach out, trailing my finger over her lush lips.

"I'm glad." I kiss the top of her head, and then tighten my arm around her, closing my eyes. "I love you." Every time I say it, there is this rush in my chest, this big feeling that I can't describe as anything but the feeling of things being right, this is right.

"I love you too." Her fingers slide over my side until she settles her hand, then she nuzzles against the side of my breast, stirring feelings inside me already again. "Sleep tight." Her voice is already slow and low, still sexy.

"Sweet dreams." I smile, trying to ignore the energy rushing through me. Trying to ignore the rush.

I've got her here in my arms, this is real. This really happened.

She loves me.

When I wake up, Sanne isn't in the bed with me anymore and for a moment I'm confused. She was here when I went to sleep. But then the door to the bedroom opens and she comes back into the room, wearing my bathrobe.

When she sees me awake, she smiles sweetly. "Good morning."

I reach out to her and she drops the bathrobe, exposing her beautiful and naked body, taking my hand. "Good morning. Did you sleep well?" I take her in my arms under the covers, enjoying the feeling of being so close to her, this contact of skin to skin. This feels so good, so right.

"Best I've slept in a long time." She sounds so contend, so happy.

"Good." I give her a soft kiss, but then she pulls back a little. "Hmm?"

"I heard voices downstairs, I think some of the others are up already." She sounds like that's a problem, but at the same time, she plays her fingers over my skin, like she may be in the mood for something else too. Mixed signals, much?

"I wouldn't be surprised. They're adults, though, they

can feed themselves." I lean in and give her a soft kiss. "I like having you with me. Here in my arms."

"I like being here." Her voice is quiet. "I did mean what I said last night. That wasn't just lust talking." She doesn't sound so sure now.

"I know. I meant it too, even if it took me a long time to realise it." I kiss her again, trying to get her to smile again. "I. Love. You." I punctuate each word with a kiss, and Sanne almost giggles.

She looks at me, her eyes sparkling. "I love you too." She gives me a hard kiss, and then really pulls back from me. "The others may be able to feed themselves, but I'm hungry too..." She eyes me and I grin at her.

"Fine, let's get some food into you." I kiss her back before I sit up. "Do you want to wear a pair of my sweats?" I crawl out of bed, going over to my closet. I don't feel much like getting dressed in nice clothes right now, I'd rather just lounge around for a while.

Sanne pads over to me, and then I feel her body pressed against me, her breasts against my back, her arms around my waist, her chin on my shoulder. "Yeah. I'm not sure if I'm awake enough to get back into a bra or tight jeans again." Her fingers start sliding up towards my breasts, moving in small increments on their way, heating up the skin where she touches it.

"Tight jeans?" I grab two pairs of my sweats and shirts, trying not to get too distracted by her fumbling and teasing.

"You didn't think those jeans were an accident, did you?" She takes my breasts in her hands, playing the job of bra, as her voice tickles my neck.

"I wasn't thinking very much at all last night," I admit. Then I turn around, smiling at her. "We can get dressed and get something to eat downstairs or we can play around here for a while, but you're going to have to decide."

She pretends like that's a hard choice but then she grins at me. "Food first. I saw that you have a pretty big shower, so I think that we can combine fun and function later." She takes one pair of sweats and a shirt and quickly puts them on.

I also put mine on and then give her a pair of very fluffy and soft socks. "So your feet won't freeze off on the tiling downstairs."

She keeps smiling, just so happy and comfortable, and I want to take her back in my arms. I want to hold her all day. Now I've finally got her, I want to keep her. It feels so silly, like some caveman kind of thing, but this feeling inside, it only gets better when I hold her close. When I keep her with me, when I kiss her and touch her...

But we're going to have to eat something first. Although, I'm not really that hungry, still pretty full from last night. But I should probably eat even if just a little.

I give Sanne a quick kiss before I take her hand and pull her out of the bedroom. "Let's satisfy that food-hunger first, before we satisfy other types of hunger."

Sanne's laugh behind me makes me feel all tingly inside and I know that this is right. This is how it's supposed to be.

19

Sanne

Everyone shoots us knowing looks when Josie drags me into the kitchen by my hand and my cheeks feel like they're on fire. Like it wasn't totally obvious what would happen last night, but now being faced with everyone again in the morning makes me feel very self aware and I don't know what to do, how to act. It's not a walk of shame, but more of a walk of fame, or something.

"Good morning." Kara slides a cup of coffee towards Josie before she looks at me. "What do you drink in the morning?"

"Tea, please." I slide onto one of the chairs at the kitchen counter. I can hear more voices in the living room, but this feels a little safer, with just Kara, Loes and Eline here, though they're all looking at me.

Josie slides on the chair next to mine, putting her hand on my arm. "What do you want to eat?" She looks at me.

I shake my head. "I think I'll have to think about that for a moment. Something to drink is enough right now."

Kara puts on the electric kettle for water for the tea before she opens the fridge. "We have a lot of leftovers, if you're hungry."

I shake my head, my stomach not agreeing with the idea of anything we ate last night, I'm not up to any of that yet.

Then Kara grins before pulling something from the freezer. "We were about to make buns and croissants and such. Don't worry, we're not having you eat salmon or stew for breakfast." She checks the cupboard over the counter before turning back to me. "Any preference for tea?"

"Black or earl grey?" I have no idea what Josie has here, I don't think I've seen her drink tea, not much anyway.

"You're in luck. She's got earl grey." Kara plucks a bag from the cupboard and, after taking the wrapper off, puts it in a glass mug before she pours over the hot water. Then she puts the glass in front of me, with a small bowl next to it, for when I take the bag back out. "You choose how you like it."

I nod. "Thanks." I look down at the tea, avoiding people's gaze.

"Anyone got a hangover?" Josie's voice is bright next to me, way brighter than I would expect.

I hear Loes laugh. "Yeah, Jurre drank too much, he didn't feel too well when he woke up."

"I don't think I count, much." I look up at Eline, at her reluctant voice, but she seems pretty good. "Not sure if it's just the long night we had or the alcohol. Just feeling a little rough." She shrugs.

"You'll feel better after some food." Kara puts the buns and croissants into the oven, closing it, and then she leans back. "Okay, time to get to the elephant in the room." She looks at Josie and me, her eyes filled with wicked joy. "Are you, or aren't you?"

"Are we, what?" Josie deadpans, but I can see how she's trying not to grin.

"Having sex? Together? Something like that?" Kara rolls her eyes.

Josie looks at me, smiling sweetly. "Are we, any of those?"

I nod, my cheeks heating up again. "Yeah, we are." I can't help my own grin, my heart filled with so many emotions that it's hard to figure out which ones.

"Care for any explanation on which one?" Kara doesn't seem fully satisfied, narrowing her eyes are Josie.

"Nope." Josie just grins at her. "That's what you get for being nosey." Then she slides her arm around me and puts her head on my shoulder. "This feels nice."

"Did you sleep enough?" I try to look at Josie, but that's not easy from this angle.

"Yeah, I did." I hear her laugh.

Then there are a lot of noises and Eline's girlfriend, Anoek, opens the door to the living room and Bente and

Tys rush into the kitchen, their noses against our legs immediately, wanting attention.

I laugh as I reach down to pet them. This feel good, this feels right.

I think I could wake up with Josie every morning, and being greeted by Bente...

All of this, it feels right.

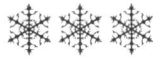

The others have finally left, the house much more quiet now, and we're sitting on the couch in the living room, under a blanket. There is something on the TV, though I'm not even sure if we're watching or if it's just background noise.

Josie moves a little, sitting up more. "Are you good with staying here for dinner?" I feel her eyes on me as I nod.

"Yeah. I don't have anything to return to, not really. And I'm not sure you can eat those leftovers all on your own." I grin at her, and she flashes me a grin back.

"I agree with you on that second observation." She lets out a breath, her eyes going more serious, almost more nervous. "Do you want to sleep over too? You can, if you want to."

I nod again, my heart beating loudly. "Yeah, I'd like that." I take a deep breath, nervous conversations are hard. "But I will have to get clean clothes and stuff like that at my place at some point. And next week, I'll have to get back to work." I don't even know why I mention it...

Josie leans closer. "I can work with that. I'll have to get back to work tomorrow anyway, since Loes can't come in at the moment. So I won't even be here most of the day." She takes my hand. "You can spend the rest of your 'holiday' hanging out here, if you want to."

"You don't mind?"

She shakes her head, smiling. "I don't mind, I'd love it. Knowing that I'll be returning to you after work." Her cheeks colour a little. The things she gets all shy over...

"I think I can stay a couple more days. I'll go pick up a few things from home tomorrow." I grin, heat coursing through my body at the thought of spending every night in the same bed as Josie.

"Good." She smiles and then pushes me back onto the couch, leaning over me. "That means I can keep doing this as much as I want, right?" She kisses me, first short kisses, teasing kisses.

"Yes." I grin, wrapping my arms around her, and her kisses get longer, deeper, more intense, sparking even more heat inside me.

If I'm staying here, we can keep doing kisses, lots of kisses, lots of touches and kisses.

My heart swells each time, with every kiss, with every caress, it keeps growing, filling with emotions, filling with love.

I may not read things like romance novels, but I'm pretty sure that this is what they describe, this feeling of love, the emotions. I've found it, even though I never expected to ever feel so intensely, to ever again feel this intensely, to feel this strongly. I do.

Maybe teenager-me was right, that this feeling was so strong that I didn't know what to do with it at the time, and now I do. Now I can handle it and actually appreciate it for what it is.

I love Josie with all my heart and want to spend every moment for the rest of my life with her.

I wrap my arms around Josie, pulling her close before I give her a slow kiss. It's really cold outside, there is still some snow on the ground, thought not that much anymore, even though it's still freezing.

It's Sunday evening and I'm going home. I've been at Josie's place all week, but I need to get back to work tomorrow, so I have to go home now. If i stay until the morning, I'm afraid that I won't actually get to work on time, and I need to get clean clothes and all those things, so staying here isn't the best plan right now, no matter how much I would like to. I don't want to actually leave.

Josie's arms tighten around me before she breaks the kiss. "I'll miss you, you know?"

"I'll miss you too." I give her another quick kiss. "I'll talk to you again tomorrow, after work."

"Maybe you can come over for dinner? I'll try to make sure to have something here to eat." She's smiling, but I can also see the sadness in her eyes. We don't want to let go. We both don't want to let go.

"We'll have to see tomorrow. Yeah?"

"I don't know. It's New Year's tomorrow, so I'm fairly sure that you don't have to go to work the day after..." She eyes me.

I let out a sigh. "Totally forgot about that. Yeah." I grin, and she shows me the same one. "Yeah. I'll come over tomorrow after work. Of course." It's just a single day of work, so why does it feel so bothersome? Why do I not want to go?

"Good." Josie grins, giving me another kiss. "I'll make it worth your while."

"You always make it worth it, just by being here." I kiss her back. "But that does mean having to actually get home, you know?"

She nods. "I know. I just... To finally have you back, I want to make up for all the time we've missed."

My heart fills and gets heavy at the same time. "I know. But we've got a long time ahead of us. We can always make up for it." I kiss her one last time before I step back. "I should really head home."

Josie nods, letting out a deep breath. "I know. And I'll see you again tomorrow."

"Tomorrow." I nod.

"I love you." She smiles as she says the words.

"I love you too. Now, go back inside, so you don't get a cold." I make a shooing motion, but she just laughs.

"I'll get back inside after you've left." She waves at me,

obviously not moving.

I let out another deep breath. "I'm going now." I get in the car, a pretty empty car, apart from the bag with clothes and a few small things. I've moved most of my stuff back to my own place in the last week, bit by bit. It's just the clothes now. And it makes me sad to see them.

Josie steps closer, reaching out and she traces a heart on the window of the car, even tough there isn't really anything to trace in.

I smile, mouthing 'I love you' at her, as I turn the car on, and as she steps back again. I slowly drive off the grounds, on my way home. I look back, seeing Josie still standing in the snow, and she waves. I wave back, then focus on the road and on getting home safely.

The drive isn't long, but with the snow and ice still making the road dangerous in some places, especially at night, I do need to make sure I don't get into accidents and such. I actually really want to spend tomorrow, and the day after and maybe, possibly, probably, even the rest of my life with Josie.

For the last days, we've spent a lot of time just talking and thinking, about our pasts, our presents and our futures.

Before I went to Schiermonnikoog, I felt like my life stood still. That everything was standing still, not moving. I didn't feel like I was really going anywhere, apart from just 'keeping going'. But, talking to Josie, I realised that I used to have dreams. I used to want things, I used to want to do things, feel things, say things. I wanted do many things, I had dreams.

That had all sort of slowed down and stopped as I was focusing on other things, on other people, and stopped seeing where I had wanted to go myself.

But with Josie at my side, her enthusiasm, her own passion, I feel like I can do things again. I feel like I've got my dreams back, and one of the first things I need to do is to get out of this dead-end job I'm in now. I've not moved anywhere in three years, stuck at the same place for all that time. It's time that I either move up, or move on.

It's going to be scary, but with Josie here, I know that it will be worth it. Taking that chance will be worth it. Because it will make me happier, it will make me feel like I'm actually doing something.

That, and having Josie back in my life. It finally feels like things are going the way that I'd always thought that my life would go.

Josie gives me strength, she gives me courage. She's always done that for me, giving me courage, but now it's even more true.

With her by my side, I can do anything, be anyone, and no matter if she knows it or not, she's always been like that for me, that strength, that important person. She was like that when we were young, and she's like that now. She's the power that lets me do anything.

I love Josie. I love her so much.

I don't even know how to properly explain it, but I do. There are so many things that we've got ahead of us, so much time. But I know that we'll manage, because I've got her at my side.

My love, my Josie.

Love.

20

Josie

The first two weeks of the new year have gone by so fast. Working, having dinner with Sanne, spending time together, it's all gone so fast that it makes my head spin sometimes. Just remembering that she's here with me now. It's such a heady feeling. It's such an amazing feeling, a rush.

I turn the lights in my office off behind me. It's Friday evening and I'm going to pick Sanne up to go to a party at Kara's place. Kara did apply for the teaching job on the island and this week she was asked to come in for an interview and everything. She thought it went pretty well, even though she didn't really know if 'pretty well' was good enough to get the job. But it's still a cause for celebration. So we're having a small party tonight and we'll probably hear or see more next week or something.

I get into the house, and Bente immediately greets me, jumping up at me with joy and I ruffle her fur for a moment. "Yeah, yeah, girl. I'm just changing and we'll be leaving soon after that. You'll be seeing Tys soon." Not that it has been long since she saw him last, he stayed here while Kara was on the island, but she always seems extra excited when I mention his name.

The house is a little chilly and I turn the heating up a some so that it's not super cold when I get back here later tonight, hopefully, probably, with Sanne at my side. I smile as I think about that. With Sanne at my side... Like it's such a normal or natural thing for us to do.

My phone buzzes and I see that it's a message from the lady in question herself. 'Do I need to pack extra warm clothes this weekend?' She'd gotten a little cold when we went for a long walk last weekend, not expecting that she could get that cold on 'just a walk' in the near-freezing weather. She's not used to those things, although, she seems to enjoy going on these long walks with me, which is good. Right?

'Yeah, probably a good idea.' Then something flits through my head. 'And maybe an extra set, so you can leave them here, in case you need them?' My heart beats a little quicker as I go up the stairs to the bedroom. Is that too soon? It's not even been a month since we saw each other again, but at the same time, she's over here all the time and this way she doesn't have to worry about an extra set of clothes or anything...

'Are you sure?'

Am I? 'Yes. It makes sense, right?' Right? I don't know how to do these things, how they work. When are you supposed to ask these things? When are you supposed to say that someone can leave their clothes over at your place, that you've got space for them? I've never really been in a 'relationship' before. The girls I've have fun with always used to know that what we did was just being with people, being together with them to have fun, but it wasn't a 'relationship', at least they were never meant to be long-term ones. And I definitely want this thing with Sanne to be long-term, as long as can be.

'I think so.' Then I see her type again. 'Is it okay if I leave a toothbrush and shampoo over there too?'

'Yes.' Of course it is. My heart beats a little faster again, if this goes well, then it feels like she's even closer to me than she is now... When her things are everywhere in the house... She doesn't feel so far away anymore, not anymore.

I want her to be close, I want all of that. Even though this relationship thing is a totally new thing for me. I've never done it before, so I don't know how to act, or what to do. But Sanne seems fine with it. Which I see as a good sign. She doesn't make me feel weird for never having done these things before and being awkward about them, and she just accepts the strange little things I sometimes do... Although, maybe I'm just the one who thinks they're ' strange' things, I have no idea...

I take my work clothes off, quickly grabbing some nice looking clothes which don't totally smell like the clinic... Then, before I put them on, I quickly grab a nicer looking bra instead of the practical one I was wearing before. I know that I don't have the sexiest undies, and I know that Sanne doesn't care, but I still like the feeling of wearing pretty clothes when I'm seeing her.

Then I run a brush through my hair and I pull it up into a bun again. It's out of the way and a little more practical like this.

I check my phone, but Sanne hasn't sent me any more messages. I send Kara a message. 'About to leave and pick up Sanne and we'll be heading your way soon.'

I put the phone into my pocket and take one last look in the mirror. I'm not sure if the flush on my cheeks is from rushing around, or the idea of seeing Sanne... It could be either, or both, really.

I've got to go, move.

I glance around my bedroom one last time, hoping I didn't leave it too much of a mess, and then I go back down the stairs, grabbing my jacket and Bente's leash. I grab my bag and leave the house again. I think I've been in the house for under ten minutes or something. But I've got to keep moving...

I open the trunk of my car and Bente immediately jumps in, sitting down on her blanket, which is already there for her. "Be a good, girl." I give her a kiss on her head before I close the trunk again and go around the side to the front of the car.

Then I get in and drive off, my thoughts on what will be happening the rest of the evening, the rest of the weekend... My stomach is still doing that butterfly and flip thing when I think of seeing Sanne again, and I wonder if that will ever go away... If that feeling ever goes away.

I hope not. I really hope that it will never go away, because I like it way too much, even if it makes me a little nervous.

I just like it so much.

When Sanne opens her door, she's grinning broadly, immediately pulling me into a hug and giving me a hard kiss. I wrap my arms around her too, holding her tight. We see each other almost every day, but we still can't seem to get enough of each other when we get near each other.

As we finally come up for air, I can't help my grin. "Hello to you too."

She winks at me and then turns around. "I just need to get a bag into the car, and then I'm ready to go."

"Good." I watch her as she turns around, she's wearing a pair of tight jeans again and a shirt that clings to all her curves, making me want to grab her and run my hands all over her...

Then, as she's bend over her bag, Sanne looks back at me, winking, shaking her ass a little.

"Showoff." I grin, stepping inside and running my hand over her amazing ass. "But we really do have to get going. Bente is a little impatient."

Sanne lets out a deep laugh as she stands up straight again, her hand on my stomach, playing her fingers over my shirt. "And you're saying that you're not showing off yourself?" She winks as she steps past me, out of the house.

I shrug, even though she can't see it. I never said that I wasn't, I do want to look good for her... But I just know that if we slow down now, that we may never get moving again, that we may never make it to Kara's place.

I follow Sanne, taking her bag to put it in the car for her, as she closes the door to the house. She lives in a very mundane neighbourhood, it's all the same type of houses, designed for a set of parents and 1,5 kids... Or something like that. I guess that there is something to say for a neighbourhood like this, but I don't know if I could ever live here, not with my love for animals and wanting a place close by to play with them, like the fields behind my house.

Sanne's hand on my back jolts me a little. "Kara just messaged me, asking where we are."

I turn around, grinning. "She's so impatient." I give Sanne a quick kiss and then we get into the car, where it's a lot warmer, luckily.

"Hello, Bente," Sanne calls out to her, looking back. And Bente lets out a short bark, moving like she wants to climb to the front, which she can't. I've put a screen behind the back row of seats since Bente is one of those dogs who will try to climb closer to you, no matter what. That wasn't safe, not for either of us... Then Sanne turns to me, her eyes shining. "I'm *so* ready for the weekend."

I start the car, smiling. "No fun at work?"

Sanne makes an unsatisfied sound. "Not really. I've been applying for new jobs and the search is going slow, but everything that just slightly annoyed me before about this place is starting to really bother me." She sighs deep. "I just want to forget about it all for a few days. I just want to enjoy myself and not have to worry about all sorts of numbers and calculations and things. Just for a weekend."

I drive out of the neighbourhood and then put my hand over hers. "I think I can make that happen. I think I can make you forget your own name, if you want to."

Sanne laughs, then she turns her hand around and takes my hand for a moment. "Thanks. I think that would be amazing. But I'm sure we've got something else to do first…"

"I know." I run my thumb over her hand, slow circles, as I turn onto the main road towards Kara's place. "But you know that if you need to talk, I'm always here for you."

"I know. I appreciate that. But I'd like to forget first, just for a few days."

"We'll make that happen." I smile. I can definitely do that, if she needs me to.

Sanne's phone starts ringing and she picks up. "Hey, Kara."

I roll my eyes, Kara is being needy. Or just being annoying. Either is possible right now.

"Yes, we're almost there. And no, I didn't distract her, not for too long, anyway. I promise." Sanne laughs. "Yes, yes. I'll tell her to hurry up."

I glance Sanne's way, who winks at me.

"We'll see you in a moment. Bye." Then she hangs up, letting out a breath as she's grinning. "I don't know what it is, but she's really excited about something and she really wants you to be there to tell you about it."

I shake my head, smiling. "She knows I'm on my way." But since Kara sounded excited, I guess that whatever it is isn't a bad thing, just a good thing.

The rest of the trip to Kara is pretty quick, she only lives a couple of minutes away from Sanne. When I park the car,

Kara is already waiting in the doorway and she comes over to the car as we're getting out.

I look at her, smiling. "Are we the first ones here?"

Kara nods, moving nervously from one foot to the other, but she's grinning more now.

"What is it?" I try to read her body language, but she's both nervous and excited, and I don't know how to understand it.

When Sanne steps next to me, Kara finally bursts. "I got the job! They just called me!" She takes a quick breath. "Ahh!"

I feel a grin pull at my cheeks as I wrap my arms around Kara. "Congratulations!" That's such great news! No wonder she's so impatient to tell people.

Then Sanne's arms are around us too. "Wow. That's so awesome!"

"I know. I know." Kara breaks free of our hugs, moving from one leg to the other again. "I can barely believe it. This is just..." Her eyes are bright and shining. "I can't believe it yet."

As I glance at Sanne, I can. Sometimes things just work out well and in unexpected ways. "I guess we're now celebrating a lot more."

"Yes." Kara nods, then she looks around, running her hands over her arms. "We should get inside. Get Bente and come inside. It's cold here." She already dashes into the house ahead of us.

I turn to Sanne, grinning. "Is that enough to make you forget things?"

She nods, then she steps closer and gives me a quick kiss. "But this is even better." She grabs my ass for a moment and then turns around and goes inside the house too, as I'm left there to let Bente out of the car, a little dazed.

As I put the leash on Bente and lock the car, I think about how things have changed so much in the last month. And how many of those changes have been so good for all of us. It's amazing how fast things can change, for the good, and often do change.

Meeting Sanne again, and now being with her... It has changed everything for me, and I feel so lucky to have her at my side.

"Josie!" Sanne calls out to me from the doorway. "Come on in! It's cold out!"

"Coming!" I wave to her as I grin.

I love her. I've always loved her. But it finally really happened.

Who says that dreams don't come true? Because mine definitely did.

Christmas dream, or wish, or not. It came true, and I've finally got the woman of my dreams.

I've finally got Sanne at my side.

My girlfriend, my heart, my love.

My everything.

Emily Engberts has been writing for years, she writes under different pen names, depending on the topic and type of story. As E. or Emmy Engberts she writes Young Adult books with queer people in them, romance novels as Emmy and scifi as E. As Rosa Swann, she was involved in the surge of the mpreg sub-genre in gay romance, and most of her work under that pen name is still gay romance. As Skylar Heart she publishes straight romance with characters who deal with difficult subjects, but still end up finding someone to love.

As Emily, she writes adult romances with queer women who won't apologise for being different and who celebrate their differences.

She is Dutch and has lived in the Netherlands for almost all her life apart from when she studied English and Creative Writing at the University of Chichester in England. This really inspired her to make writing her career and has been working towards that goal ever since.

Emily currently lives in Groningen with her partner and two cats, and if she's not writing, you can find her playing videogames or working on one of her many creative projects.

Website: www.emmyengberts.com

Printed in Great Britain
by Amazon

49347037R00118